I0598310

A Perfectly Imperfect Holiday

by

Kate Berberich

Destination Romance, Book Two

A Perfectly Imperfect Holiday

Cover Art by *Jennifer Greeff*

The Wild Rose Press, Inc.
PO Box 708
Adams Basin, NY 14410-0708
Visit us at www.thewildrosepress.com

Publishing History
First Edition, 2023
Trade Paperback ISBN 978-1-5092-5277-0
Digital ISBN 978-1-5092-5278-7

Destination Romance, Book Two
Published in the United States of America

"If you're pregnant with our kid, that kid is gonna meet all the Santas and angels and—I dunno—Easter bunnies? All the stuff me and Dylan didn't get—"

"Our kid will be loved, is what you mean. And…you mean it? 'Our kid?' "

"Well, yeah."

"It's just…you said you'd support my decision. You never said you wanted—"

He swallowed a hard lump of the past. "It was a lot to think about, you know? I never really considered…but yeah. If I helped make a kid, and you wanna have that kid…I'm not going anywhere." He leaned down and kissed her—right there in the middle of the market. After a moment there was a scattering of applause accompanied by a chorus of "oohs." They broke the kiss to more applause and quite a few camera flashes. Heat crept up his neck. Dammit. He rested his forehead on Lacey's. "They must think I just—"

"There are worse things. Just go with it." She smiled at the crowd and waggled her left hand, even though she was wearing her red wool gloves.

More applause and a few calls of "*Gefeliciteerd.*" A chubby-cheeked baker in a green-striped apron bustled out from her stall and presented them with two heart-shaped ginger cookies.

It was entirely more attention than he was comfortable with, but Lacey glowed with happiness, and that made it worthwhile.

It made a lot of things worthwhile.

Even picking up her socks off the rug every morning.

Praise

Five Stars for *Picture Imperfect*

If you're looking for the glamor of a 1940s movie set in the contemporary world, then *Picture Imperfect* is the love story for you. Two people with flaws and questionable pasts. Place them in close proximity traveling throughout Europe. The result? A wonderfully charming novel of love, trust, and second chances.
~N.N. Lights BookHeaven

Dedication

For Jill, who wanted another adventure with Dan and
Lacey.

Chapter One

"Haven't you ever seen *A Christmas Carol*? It's tradition." Dan Lewis fixed his seatmate, lover, plus-one, and all-around light of his life, Lacey Devere, with a look of profound disbelief.

"I don't care if it's tradition, I am not eating a goose!" Lacey crossed her arms and glared at him. Adorably.

But then, he found everything about her adorable, from the way her bright blue eyes sparkled when she laughed, to the way she scrunched up her face when confronted with an unfamiliar food item. Like now. Not to mention how dazzling she looked when he managed to coax her out of her jeans and sneakers and into a formal gown. Or just plain out of her jeans and sneakers.

He adjusted his position. *Probably not the best time to entertain those images...*

Around them, passengers napped, read, or perused their electronic devices. Anything to pass the time. Impeccably groomed flight attendants moved about the cabin, dispensing beverages or other small comforts.

"Have you ever tried it? Do you even know what goose tastes like?" He glared right back with the mix of affection and exasperation that was his new normal since meeting her. He secretly liked it.

"Nope, and I don't wanna know. Geese eat grass. Dogs do stuff on grass. No goose."

He scrubbed his eyes with the heels of his hands. "Those are Canadian geese, on random patches of green in New York City. These are farm-raised, right alongside the turkeys and hams."

"No, goose." She huddled in the corner of her seat, arms crossed. She pushed out her lower lip in a perfect pout, but he resisted the urge to take it between his teeth and nibble before kissing her silly.

"You know we're going to the Netherlands, Germany, and Austria, right? There's all sorts of culinary delights for you to sample—raw herring, blood sausage—"

"Please stop."

Not in the mood for teasing. Got it.

He reached for her wrist to check the time on her new watch—turnabout was fair play, after all. To his surprise, she wrapped her arm even tighter around her middle. *Okay...what's going on here?* She was paler than she'd been a moment ago and her hand was cold. He frowned and turned a bit in his seat. "Babe...Lacey...no one's gonna make you eat anything you don't want to. I'd never...trick you or anything. You know that, right?"

She nodded, her face pinched. The luxuriously padded leather seat dwarfed her.

Now she was scaring him. "Is it the plane? I thought flying didn't bother you anymore?"

A tiny head shake. "I don't...I think I'm gonna..." She lurched forward, fumbling for the airsick bag.

He bit back a swear and pulled her long blonde hair away from her face, then braced her as best he could. Between the two of them, they got most of the mess into the bag. He swallowed hard and ignored the sour odor.

Their nearest fellow passengers muttered words of varying degrees of civility. One helpful soul rang for assistance.

Lacey gasped and trembled like a leaf. "I'm sorry." She swiped at her streaming eyes. "I'm so sorry."

"Hey…calm down. Not your fault." He rubbed her back, wondering what was wrong. There was no turbulence. Dinner hadn't been served yet and she hadn't had anything to drink.

A flight attendant materialized with silent efficiency, wearing latex gloves and an apron to protect his immaculate uniform. "If you'd care to freshen up, miss, I'll get this taken care of straight away."

She wobbled to her feet, leaning heavily on his arm—which he didn't care for at all.

"I'm so—"

"No worries, miss. I'll have this tidied right up."

Another attendant waited outside the first-class lavatory with a bottle of water and a clean hand towel. "There's a dental kit on the counter if you want to clean your teeth."

Lacey mustered a watery smile. "Thanks. I'm—"

"Oy! No apologies, miss. It happens to the best of us." She shooed Lacey into the tiny cubicle. "You get tidied up and you'll feel much better."

Dan reluctantly loosened his hold on Lacey, waiting until she was steady on her feet. "All right?"

She nodded.

He leaned in and kissed her clammy forehead. "I'll be right here." He released a long, slow breath and slumped against the wall. This was definitely not how he'd envisioned the start of their first holiday season together.

****

Lacey drained the miniature bottle of mouthwash and spat the minty green glop into the sink. She splashed her face with cold water and let it run for a while, erasing all traces of her mess. What remained of her makeup was mostly smudged under her eyes.

Goodie. A genuine New York City raccoon.

Her festive cranberry red sweater that promised to make her look "glowy" made her look washed out instead.

Their first Christmas together, one of Dan's first assignments as Dolce Vita's executive security consultant, and here she was, puking her guts out at God knows how many thousand feet in the air.

So classy.

She could hear Jenny already. Doctor Darling-of-the-Society-Pages would never do anything so gauche as get airsick. She straightened her clothes and pushed her hair behind her ears, wishing for her brush. Well, she still looked like crap, but at least it was a slightly better grade of crap. She plastered a smile on her face and opened the door.

Dan's dark blue cashmere sweater and gray jeans complemented his close-shorn salt-and-pepper hair and stormy blue eyes perfectly, as always. She noticed a few speculative glances.

Yes, the whole package really is as amazing as advertised, and yes, he's really waiting for me.

He straightened from an easy slouch with his usual cat-like grace and ran his hand down her arm, cupping her elbow. "Better?" Tension etched a hard line between his eyes, and she regretted being the cause.

She nodded and manufactured a smile for him. "I'm

s—"

He laid a warm finger on her lips. "Stop it. People get airsick. It's a thing. No one blames you." He shifted his hand and cupped her cheek, stroking his thumb over her cheekbone. "You okay?"

She closed her eyes and leaned into his touch—just for a second. "I think so."

He kept a tight grasp on her waist for the short walk back to their seats. His hands were warm and strong, ensuring she was steady. Her tray table glistened with a faint hint of disinfectant. The flight attendant had left a small basket containing a bottle of ginger ale, a bag of crackers, and a couple of packets of different stomach remedies.

"See? No big deal. It happens all the time." He waited for her to settle into her seat, then resumed his own. "Did I tell you? We've got tickets for opening night of *The Nutcracker* at Covent Garden, Wednesday."

"I always wanted to see it when I was a little girl. It was way too expensive."

"Why did I not have you pegged as a ballet fan?"

She elbowed him. "Every little girl goes through a ballerina phase. And I was fascinated by the little kids dancing on such a big fancy stage."

"I don't think there's as many kids in this production, but it looks stunning. Did you pack a dress?"

"You know very well I did since we're going to an actual ball on New Year's Eve."

"The blue one you got for the opera?"

"Yeah." She yawned, just barely remembering to cover her mouth. *Let's not share the germs.* "And a couple of others."

"The sparkly little thing you wore to the club in

Madrid?"

"No. I'm trying to get past all that, remember? And anyway, you didn't have fun that night."

"But you did. I can deal with something if it makes you happy." He considered that for a moment. "Well, in small doses, anyway."

She regarded him lazily. "I'd rather do things we both enjoy. I'm growing up, remember? But if you really like that outfit, I'll pack it next time. I'm sure we'll find a way to amuse ourselves." *There. That sounds like our usual level of flirty flirt, right?* Apparently, since Dan relaxed a bit.

"Well, there's something fun we can do together when we get to Vienna. The group is booked for a dance class before the New Year's Eve ball. It's a thing—even people who live there take classes. No one makes fun of you for practicing before the big day."

She snorted. "Jenny made me and Dad take lessons so we wouldn't 'embarrass her at the wedding.' I'm good." She tried to keep the bitterness from her tone, but from the look on Dan's face, she didn't quite succeed. She pasted on a smile. "But if you want to, sure."

"We've got plenty of time to decide. What do you want to see when we get to London?"

"The big department store with the fancy food court. We didn't get there last time." Her smile deepened into something more genuine, recalling exactly what had distracted them.

"We can go there. It's spectacular for the holidays. Although you might not care for some of the things on display. Figs and raisins and candied citron are pretty popular."

"Yuck." She elbowed him again, eliciting another

rich, smoky chuckle. That sound still sent pleasant shivers rippling up her spine.

Dan lifted her hand to his lips and pressed a gentle kiss to the back of it. "Why don't you take a nap? I'll wake you when we get close. You've never seen London from the air." He lowered their hands to the armrest, rubbing his thumb gently over her fingers.

She relaxed and let the cushy leather seat engulf her. "So much for our perfect romantic first Christmas."

He gave her hand a little shake. "Hey—we're together. That's all I need for it to be perfect. Rest, now."

She squeezed his hand and let her eyes flutter shut. After a moment, she felt Dan shifting around beside her, then the comforting weight of his jacket settled over her. She inhaled the familiar scents of leather and sandalwood and something uniquely *Dan,* and her lips curled in a contented smile. The last thing she recalled before she drifted off was his warm lips pressed to her temple.

Chapter Two

Evergreen garlands tied with red velvet bows adorned the hotel lobby, spicing the air with a crisp, woodsy scent. A lush Norway spruce decorated with shining red and gold baubles soared through the atrium and staff members sported jaunty holly boutonnieres. Enormous baskets brimmed with new toys destined for a children's charity. It was a masterpiece of elegant holiday festivity, except for one rather glaring detail.

"Please check again." Dan glanced at Lacey, curled into one of the plush golden velvet lobby chairs, looking too pale and glassy-eyed for his taste.

"I'm sorry, sir, but we haven't a reservation for Mr. Lewis or Ms. Devere."

The tour host sweated in his impeccable teal uniform and starched white shirt. He must have seen the company newsletter announcing Dan's hire—by none other than new owner Henry Wilson himself. He leaned across the counter. "I'm sure you can find something for one of Dolce Vita's elite guests. This is a splendid property, and it would be a shame if it were dropped from our preferred vendor list."

The desk clerk gulped, no doubt seeing stacks of American dollars evaporating before his eyes. "Of course. Let's get your guest settled, and you and I can sort the paperwork after."

"Excellent."

Dan tuned them out momentarily, scanning the lobby for exits and security cameras. The doormen in their top hats and white gloves were window dressing, but those two fellows in hunter-green blazers cruising the lobby were professional security. He'd note all those details in his assessment of the property. He glanced at Lacey with a small smile, then returned his attention to the drama unfolding in front of him.

The desk clerk did more desk clerk things, then waved over the bellman in charge of their luggage and handed him a key pack. "Our apologies for the delay, Mr. Lewis. Andrew will show you to your room."

Dan nodded his thanks and offered Lacey a hand up. "You okay, babe?"

"Yeah. Just a bit tired. I really want to lie down and take a nap."

That wasn't like her. Dan fought to keep his mouth from settling into a frown. "You will." He slipped an arm around her shoulders and kissed her temple. "Promise."

They followed the bellman into an elevator, rode up a few flights, and walked down a hallway carpeted in elegant green and gold. He stopped at a room and checked the number against the key pack in his hand. A Do Not Disturb tag hung on the doorknob. Moans and ecstatic cries were audible through the door. Dan and Lacey exchanged glances. Neither of them understood the language spoken in the room, but the message was pretty clear. Not to mention the rhythmic thudding of the headboard against the wall.

Sweat beaded the poor fellow's face, and his ears flamed scarlet. "Er…if you'll excuse me a moment." He stepped aside and tapped a button on his headset, whispering urgently into the mic.

Dan merely raised an eyebrow. Lacey scrunched her eyes shut and knocked her head against his shoulder.

The bellman returned. "I do beg your pardon, sir, madam. We'll just step down to the end of the corridor. If you'll follow me?"

"It's fine. Stuff happens." He'd prefer if it wasn't happening to them, but it wasn't the bellman's fault, and he didn't want to be the villain of the next six months' worth of watercooler gossip.

Andrew led them to another door and unlocked it with his master key. He opened the door with a flourish and flicked on the lights.

And stopped dead in his tracks. The room was a disaster. The plush green carpet was a minefield of bedding and used towels, the refrigerator door hung open, and dirty dishes littered every possible surface. A whiff of stale cigarette smoke drifted out.

Lacey pressed a hand to her mouth and stepped back.

Dan inhaled sharply, then exhaled the tension. Or tried to. "Look, I know this isn't your fault, but we're jetlagged, and my...friend was ill on the plane, so if you could just find us a clean, unoccupied room, that would be swell." He wasn't quite ready to play the "I know the owner" card, but it wasn't far off.

Lacey quirked an eyebrow at his word choice, then sagged against his shoulder. He pressed his lips to the crown of her head and rubbed her back soothingly.

"Of course, sir." Andrew stepped aside and carried on another harried conversation with the front desk.

His voice rose, and Dan looked over, raising an inquisitive eyebrow.

"What—really? Blimey. Does my key even work up

there? All right, I'll be right there." He turned to Dan and Lacey. Sweat oozed down his face, which was currently a shade of red, verging on purple. "If you'll follow me?"

Lacey scrubbed a hand over her eyes but followed him to the elevator. Dan kept his peace and let her lean against him—at least until he noticed which way the numbers were ticking.

"Why are we going down?"

Andrew gulped, then plastered a smile on his face. "We're relocating you to the penthouse, sir, to apologize for the confusion. We're going to the lobby because I don't have a key for the private lift. Your butler will meet us there."

Dan's eyes narrowed. *Butler?* "There's not a reality TV show being filmed here, is there?"

"No, sir! We'd never permit—"

Lacey laid a hand on his arm. "Dan."

He huffed out a sigh, then dug a few pounds out of his wallet and passed them over. "Sorry, kid. It's been a long day. I know none of this is your fault."

"I really do apologize, sir. This isn't the sort of thing that goes on here." He gulped. "Usually."

The elevator door swished open, admitting a wash of genteel instrumental holiday carols. A portly gentleman, resplendent in a green and black uniform complete with a striped waistcoat and a watch and chain awaited them. "Sir, madam, I am Mr. Briggs, the chief butler. On behalf of the management, I apologize most sincerely for the confusion with your reservation. If you would be so good as to follow me?"

Still looking around for a film crew, Dan guided Lacey out of the elevator—and right back into the one next to it. This one had a discreet plaque engraved "private" in elegant script and a keycard reader instead of a call button. A hunter-green velvet bench stretched across the back of the elevator car, and Lacey flopped onto it, keeping hold of his hand.

Andrew pushed in the polished brass luggage trolly, standing almost at attention in the presence of the butler. The car glided to the top floor and opened into a smaller but no less opulent version of the main lobby. Lacey brightened and squeezed his hand when she spotted the two life-sized nutcrackers flanking the gleaming concierge desk. There was nothing so crass as a uniformed security guard in plain sight here, but Dan had no doubt whatsoever there was a concealed panic button on the business side of the glossy mahogany desk. He'd investigate later and add it to his file.

Mr. Briggs nodded to Andrew. "The Princess Beatrice Suite, if you please."

A smiling woman dressed in an old-fashioned maid's uniform swung open a pair of polished wooden doors at the end of the corridor. She looked like an extra from one of those historical dramas in her black dress, white apron, and cap. Still, the effect was charming.

"This is Mrs. Patel, your housekeeper. She will assist you with any requests regarding your accommodations." He passed Dan a key pack. "This will access the private elevator, as well as your suite. There is a billiard room and reading room exclusively for our penthouse guests, and of course, you may have anything you wish delivered from the pantry, kitchen, or lobby shops at any time. You may reach a butler via the hotel's app using any of your electronic devices twenty-four hours a day."

Andrew took their luggage through to what Dan

presumed was the bedroom. It was a little hard to tell. All the hotels Dolce Vita frequented were the height of luxury but this…this was in a class by itself.

A Christmas tree sparkling with red and gold glass baubles divided the open space into separate sitting and dining areas. Lacey made a beeline for a couch upholstered in cream brocade and piled high with hunter-green and crimson velvet cushions trimmed with gold fringe. She unlaced her boots and curled her feet under herself with a blissful sigh. A gas fire burned merrily behind shining glass doors. Velvet stockings that matched the cushions hung from the mantel and a festive arrangement of greenery and red roses perfumed the air.

Dan cupped her face in his hand. She smiled at him, and he kissed the top of her head. "I'm gonna have a hard time getting you up from there, aren't I?"

She snuggled deeper into her nest of pillows. "All I need is a cat."

He rolled his eyes. *A cat. Trust Lacey to want the impossible.* "You're probably out of luck on that score."

Mrs. Patel looked up from hanging their jackets in the entryway. "Well, actually—"

"You're kidding!" Lacey straightened, glancing wide-eyed over the back of the couch.

"Not at all, miss. We've an arrangement with a local rescue agency. Guests may borrow a cat for the duration of their stay. Only on this floor, of course."

"Of course." Dan chuckled. He eyed Lacey, who chewed her lip. He'd do it, too—anything to make this holiday perfect for her.

Anything to forget the mess from Italy…

****

Lacey sank into the luxurious pile of cushions. A cat

to cuddle would be lovely—of course, it would, but—

"It doesn't seem fair to the cats…letting them think they have a home, then sending them back."

The housekeeper bustled about, adjusting lights and drapes. She had a motherly smile and a musical lilt to her voice. "Well, between you and me, miss, a lot of them are adopted by the staff once their guests leave. So everyone gets their happily ever after."

Lacey pulled one of the cushions into her lap and rested her chin on it, playing with the tassels. "We're only here for a few days. We won't really have time to spend with a cat."

"Of course, miss. Shall I unpack for you?"

"No, thanks. We've got it," Dan assured her.

The corner of Lacey's mouth quirked up. She knew he was itching for privacy to do his usual security walk.

"Perhaps a nice pot of tea while you're settling in?" Mrs. Patel pulled an incongruous top-of-the-line smartphone from the pocket of her white, ruffled apron and opened an app.

Lacey wrinkled her nose. *Ugh. Cups of dead leaves again.* Her stomach gave an unpleasant little lurch. "Maybe some soup and toast?" She glanced at Dan. "You should have a solid meal, though. Did you eat on the plane?"

"I didn't want the smell to bother you," he admitted.

Mrs. Patel glanced between the two of them. "If your stomach is unsettled from traveling, the chef can prepare something bland—roast chicken and mashed potatoes?"

Mr. Briggs cleared his throat. Lacey saw Andrew pushing the now-empty trolly into the hallway. "Or we could secure dinner reservations at the restaurant of your choice," the butler suggested.

Lacey pushed aside her pillow.

Suck it up. This is Dan's trip, too, and if he wants a nice dinner, you will get up and get dressed—

"We may take you up on that another evening," Dan cut in smoothly. "Right now, we'd just like some quiet time."

Mr. Briggs nodded impassively and followed the bellman.

Dan smiled at Mrs. Patel. "Something simple for supper would be perfect."

She nodded and made a few notes on her phone. "Of course. Thirty minutes?"

"Excellent." He walked her to the door.

The door clicked shut out in the foyer, followed by silence. Lacey snuggled into her cozy nest, too comfy to think about moving. Dan returned to the sitting area, silent on socked feet, and rested his hands on the back of the couch, leaning over her.

"Someday you're gonna show me all the things you check for in a new room."

He kissed her cheek, then rested his forehead against hers. "Someday," he agreed. "Just not today."

"There's a camera at the elevators. And a fire exit next to the concierge desk."

"Good eyes. Place this big, we might even have our own private fire exit. Why don't you rest until the food comes?"

She nodded, blinking groggily. Dan still seemed tense, even now that they were settled in their room. Why wasn't he relaxing? She was so tired…just a little nap, then she'd ferret it out of him…

"Do you want a blanket?"

Her mouth curved in a sleepy smile. "No. Just you."

"Not going anywhere. I promise." He kissed the end of her nose, then straightened and stepped away.

Chapter Three

Andrew had left their bags in the passage between the bedroom and bath. Dan wasn't sure if it was properly called a dressing room or a walk-through closet. It was bigger than some of the bedrooms he'd had when he was a kid. Their suitcases were set on stands flanking two bureaus. His suit bag and Lacey's dress bag were hung up in the space opposite.

He set up his laptop on one of the bureaus and opened a video chat with his sister, then eyed the suitcases. His, he knew was perfectly neat and orderly. Lacey's was just as likely to explode like one of those spring snakes in a can. He opted to deal with his own bag first.

The session connected, and Dylan's smiling face filled the screen. "Danny!" She got a glimpse of the space behind him and frowned. "Why are you calling me from inside the closet?"

He turned the computer so she could see the scale of the space. "Mix up with our reservations, so we were upgraded to the penthouse."

"Whoa. Swanky much. Where are you?"

"London."

"Get me some of those good chocolate bars, would you? You forgot last time."

"I didn't forget; I got distracted."

"You mean, you fell in love."

17

He opened his mouth, then shut it. There was a time, not so long ago, when he would have scoffed at the notion. Now…his hand felt empty without Lacey's fingers curled around his. His world felt a little colder when she wasn't there. He didn't sleep as well without her. A soft smile played over his features. "Yeah, I guess I did."

"I'm glad." She cocked her head to one side, studying him. "Have you told her yet?"

The smile dissolved and his face heated. He wasn't good at this sort of thing. Never had been.

Dylan's expression softened. "I know you care, or you wouldn't be with her. I'm sure you show her, every day, in a million little ways."

"I try."

She nodded. "I know you do. And I know you two aren't very traditional, but it's nice to hear the words."

He set a neatly folded stack of shirts in a drawer and closed it. "I'll take your word for that."

"I like her. You smile more when she's around." She paused, frowning, "Well, usually. You're not smiling now. What's wrong?"

Crap. She noticed. Of course, she did.

He grimaced, then smoothed it into a smile.

On-screen, Dylan rolled her eyes. "Nice try, big bro. What's wrong?"

"Lacey got a little airsick on the flight over, that's all."

She snickered. "And did you join in the puke party?"

"No, I did not. Someone in my checkered past gave me a lot of practice in controlling my gag reflex."

"Are you sure? You seem kinda tense for something that can be fixed with some meds from the airport shop."

He selected a pair of jeans from his bag, refolding them before placing them in a drawer. "I'm fine. Really. I'm a bit jetlagged and worried about Lacey and then the adventures getting our room." He reached into the suitcase again.

"Keep telling yourself that." Then her lips twisted into another smirk, eyes sparkling. "Something you want to tell me, Danny? That doesn't look like quite your style."

He glanced down. The item in his hands wasn't his, it was Lacey's *Water Lilies* shirt from Paris, along with a pair of filmy pink panties. Heat crept up the back of his neck. "She had to leave in the middle of a tour for her sister's wedding. She forgot a couple of things." He folded the T-shirt around the little scrap of pink and shoved it into a drawer.

Lacey padded up behind him. She was practicing her sneaking, but he was a professional sneak, so he didn't flinch when she threaded her arms around his waist and rested her cheek against his arm. "Or maybe I didn't want you to forget about me."

"Not very likely." His lips twitched with a smile that threatened to overtake his patented "grumpy older brother" mien.

Dylan smirked and winked at Lacey.

"Hi, Dylan."

"Hey, Lacey. How're you doing? Danny said you got sick on the plane."

"It's nothing. I hope. I popped antacids by the handful the whole time I was home for Jenny's wedding."

He twisted his head and peered at her. "You didn't tell me that."

She shrugged. "It's nothing. Just nerves or whatever."

"Family can be tough," Dylan commiserated. "Especially a wedding, with all the details and drama."

"You have no idea." Lacey gave him a little squeeze. "I'm gonna freshen up a bit before the food gets here."

"You want me to unpack your stuff?"

"If I say I'll just live out of my bag for the next couple of days, your eye is gonna twitch every time you walk through here, isn't it?"

Dylan smothered a snort, and Dan shot her a sour look.

Lacey snickered. "Fine. Just don't peek at your presents."

****

Dan bent and stroked a loose golden curl back from Lacey's face. He brushed his lips against her temple, partly because kissing her was one of his favorite things, partly to see if she had a fever. She didn't feel feverish, but he kissed her a second time, to be sure. "Come on…bed."

"Mmmff…comfy."

"You'll be comfier in bed." If anything, she settled deeper into the cushions. He chuckled and scooped her into his arms. He worked out—well, until the last couple of weeks, anyway. He was in decent shape, but tiny as she was, most of her weight was muscle. At least the bedroom wasn't far. He laid her on the bed and nudged her shoulder. "Hey—PJs." She made another incoherent little noise, and he pressed the soft cotton sleep shirt— printed with cats perpetrating various forms of holiday mischief—into her hands. "You just have to get up for a few minutes to change. You'll be more comfortable."

Helping her undress might be one of his favorite activities, but he absolutely refused to do it without her explicit permission—and jetlag plus medhead did not equal consent. Not by a long shot.

He grabbed his own sleepwear and ducked into the bathroom. When he returned, Lacey was curled under the covers…and her sweater, jeans, and assorted other items were tossed in a haphazard pile on a green brocade wing chair. He shook his head with a small smile tugging at his lips and switched off the lights.

He slid into bed and let the crisp, clean sheets envelope him. Lacey snuggled against him, and he slid an arm over her waist. A hint of lavender tickled his nose. This was what he'd been missing while she was in New York dealing with Jenny's wedding. Never mind that they were in a hotel room an ocean away from where either of them was born…if Lacey was in his arms, he was home. Maybe it should have scared him, how quickly she'd taken up residence in his heart, but like everything else about her, this just felt…right. He rested his chin on her hair, and rubbed his thumb lightly over soft cotton, warm with her body heat.

"I'm sorry," she murmured drowsily.

He kissed her hair. "What for, babe?"

"I'm not feeling very sexy right now."

He frowned in the darkness. "So?"

"Isn't that the proper grand romantic thing when you've been separated? A night of wild, passionate sex?"

A hint of laughter overlaid the weariness in her voice, and he relaxed. And responded in kind.

"For one thing, you're always sexy." His tone turned serious. "For another, this…us…isn't…transactional. We'll have plenty of wild, passionate sex…on your

21

terms."

"You're sure you don't mind?"

"Positive."

She pulled his arm tighter around her and cuddled it. "This, right now, is pretty perfect."

"It is." He pressed his lips to the crown of her head again. "Rest, now."

****

Lacey scrunched her eyes shut and burrowed into her pillows, but there was no escaping the bolt of bright golden light shining through the chink in the green brocade drapes. *Wait…light? What time was it, anyway?* She leaned up on one elbow, and a tangle of hair flopped over her eyes. Her mouth tasted like something had crawled in there and died.

Dan brushed the hair back from her face. "Morning, gorgeous." He'd already showered and dressed and sat against the headboard, working on his laptop.

"G'morning, handsome. What time z'it?"

"Around eleven, local time."

"What?" She forced herself upright, out of the cozy nest of covers. "Why didn't you wake me? The tour—"

He shut the computer and set it on the nightstand. "For one thing, most of the stuff on this tour is at night, for the lights. And even if it wasn't, how many times were you up last night? And how much stomach medication did you take?"

She scrubbed a hand over her face. "Crap. I'm sorry. I didn't mean to—"

"I don't care that you woke me; I care that you won't tell me what's wrong."

"I…honestly, I thought it was just nerves and aggravation from the wedding. Still do, really." She nestled into his side, and he slid an arm around her. "I missed you, and I thought once we were together and I was away from Jenny and all her drama, I'd be fine."

Dan combed through her bedhead with his clever fingers. "I thought I'd make it worse if I went with you."

A huff of mirthless laughter escaped her lips. "Trust me, there was plenty of commentary. I missed you so much, but even I know it's rude to make a production of introducing your new significant other at someone else's wedding. I tried so hard to just…stay out of the way and not make waves."

"To not be yourself?"

"Pretty much."

He pulled her close, and she reveled in the steady thrum of his heartbeat beneath her cheek.

"It could just be wedding drama and jetlag, but I want you to promise me if it doesn't clear up in a day or so, you'll get checked out."

She nodded against his soft linen shirtfront. "I promise."

He pressed his lips to the crown of her head.

"I should get up," she mumbled.

"There's no rush."

"I don't want to waste the day."

"Lacey, I work for the tour company and the owners are pretty fond of you. We can come back whenever we want."

"But—"

"And I'd really like you to eat something more substantial than a slice of toast and two spoonfuls of potatoes stolen off my plate." He gave her a gentle squeeze. "Come on—eat, and if you're feeling all right, we'll go on the bus tonight to see the lights."

"A company bus, all sealed inside climate-controlled glass?"

"As opposed to?"

She grabbed his arm, bouncing a little with excitement. "One of those big red ones, where you can sit on top."

"And get rained on and chilled?"

She sat up and grinned, and she could see his resolve draining away. "I've got a coat. And a nice warm plus-one." She wrinkled her nose.

That sounds so cheesy.

"All right, but only if you eat. Deal?"

"Deal. But nothing weird. No burned tomatoes or dead fishies or funky local sausages that look like a pile of—"

"Lacey, I'll order you a cheeseburger if you'll eat it."

Her stomach clenched and gurgled at that idea. *Where'd I leave that bottle of the pink stuff?* "Maybe a plate of fries? Or more of those yummy mashed potatoes?"

"Got it. Spuds for one." He grabbed his phone.

"Did you eat yet? Make sure you get something for yourself."

He made a noncommittal noise as he fiddled with an app.

"Dan."

He looked up from the screen.

"This whole you and me thing, it works both ways, you know." She traced a furrowed line on his forehead with her fingertips. "What's bothering you?"

"It's nothing."

"Dan."

He sighed and caught her hand, kissing her palm, then the pulse point of her wrist. "I missed you. And I'm still getting used to this whole legitimate career thing, okay?"

"But you'd tell me, right? We're partners—that's what you said when you asked me to be your plus-one."

"I know. I meant it. I just…I've been on my own for so long…I'm still figuring out how to be with someone else."

"I know." She brushed a kiss to his jaw. "Can I add one more thing to the list?"

"Like what?"

"Like what are we calling ourselves? Boyfriend and girlfriend sounds like 'will you be my date for prom.' Friends sounds like we're covering up for something—"

"And lovers is none of anyone's damn business. You know, we could call ourselves Dan and Lacey. Just saying."

"Yeah. We could."

****

Lacey checked her reflection one last time and added another swipe of blush to each cheek. *At least I don't look like I'm about to keel over*. The oversized holly-green sweater and heavy black leggings were hardly glamorous, but she'd be warm. She stuck her head out of the dressing room.

"Did you get the tickets for the bus tour?"

"Doing it right now. Are you sure you don't want to take the Dolce Vita bus?"

"Very. Does your tux need to be pressed?" She selected two dresses from her garment bag and carried them to the sitting area, where Dan was engrossed in his laptop. "Babe? Tux?"

"Yeah, it should probably get pressed or steamed or whatever it is they do."

"Which dress for the ballet?" She held up the glittery ice-blue gown Mrs. Wilson bought for her in Vienna and a sleek midnight-blue satin cocktail dress.

Dan looked over, and a low whistle escaped his lips. "Is that new?"

"I got it in New York."

"Well, there's no official dress code at Covent Garden. Which do you like better?"

She chewed her bottom lip. "It's not a question of what I like. Which is more appropriate?"

He pushed the computer aside and focused on her. "They're both beautiful, and you'll be stunning either way. But if you really want my opinion, wear the sparkly one."

"Really? It's not too much?"

"Really. It's Christmas, and you're meant to shine."

She draped the dresses over a chair and crossed the room to the table where he sat. He wrapped one arm around her waist, and she kissed the top of his head.

"What are you working on?"

He pulled the laptop closer. "Mr. Wilson is thinking of investing in a fleet of top-of-the-line double-decker motor coaches for the company. He wants to compete with these guys." He turned the screen so she could see the screenshots of a luxury double-decker bus. Instead of being open, the top level was glass-enclosed. It was fitted with small tables and chairs instead of the usual rows of seats.

"Okay, that's very cool, but what were you really working on before you changed tabs?"

To anyone else, Dan probably appeared unfazed.

Lacey saw a small muscle jump in his jaw. Her eyes narrowed. "You never did tell me about the rest of your trip. Did something happen after I left?"

"I'm beginning to wish I'd gone with you." He scrubbed his eye with the heel of his hand.

"Nah…too much drama. You'd have been miserable."

He grabbed one of her hands and kissed it. "I was miserable without you." There was a weariness to his voice, and Lacey caught it.

"Right. Miserable on the Amalfi Coast. I know you're worried about something. I wish you'd tell me."

"I didn't want to upset you." His shoulders slumped. "Especially when you're not feeling well."

"See, keeping secrets is exactly the sort of thing that's guaranteed to upset me. Spill." She laid her hands on his shoulders and squeezed gently. He made a sound like a tomcat purring, so she applied a bit more pressure, kneading the tense muscles.

"There was a robbery. Great way to start my brand-new legitimate career."

"Hey—these things happen. It's why you were hired." He didn't reply. "What else? Come on—tell me."

"The woman says the thief was part of the tour group. Or wearing a teal wristband, at any rate."

"Okay. Why's this bothering you so much?"

"The victim said…she met him at a hotel pool. Then they went to her room. They—or at least she—had quite a bit to drink. When she woke the next morning, he was gone. So was her diamond tennis bracelet and earrings."

"But the company literature says to leave the real jewelry at home."

"I know. I made them put that in."

"So? She did something stupid and got robbed. I don't see how—"

"That's a bit harsh."

She sighed. "I don't mean it to be. I'm sorry it happened—of course I am. And I'm sorry it affects you."

"You don't sound convinced."

"There are about a million PSAs about this sort of thing—keep an eye on your drink, be aware of your surroundings, and be super careful who you take to your room." She kissed his cheek, then rested her chin on his shoulder, looping her hands loosely around his neck. "What else?"

"She was robbed by a handsome man wearing a Dolce Vita wristband whom she met in one of the hotel pools. Sound like anyone you know?"

"No, it doesn't." Lacey straightened and pushed at his shoulder until he faced her. She grabbed his hands and held on tight. "It was a stupid and obvious theft. You'd never—"

He huffed out a mirthless laugh. "But how do I explain that? Also, you know—a decent-looking man wearing a teal wristband who likes to swim."

"Just 'decent-looking?' Not devastatingly handsome?" She gave his hands a playful shake. "Now I know it wasn't you."

"I was being modest." He produced a vague approximation of a smile for her. "Devastatingly handsome, huh?"

She squeezed his hands again. "Who would never, ever do anything like this. Wait—did someone actually accuse you?"

He shook his head wearily. "No. It was a roof-top pool with a swim-up bar. The victim had already been drinking when she met him. By the time she gave her statement, she was too hung over to describe the thief besides 'handsome.' That's not enough for a formal accusation. Not without inviting an ugly lawsuit."

"But?"

"But if asked, I have no one to confirm I was, in fact, asleep in my own room."

"Because I was in New York."

Dan pulled her into his lap. "Hey—this is not your fault."

"Well, it's not yours either." She wrapped her arms around his neck. "The company brochure says not to bring valuables. It warns about pickpockets. It shouldn't have to spell out to grown adults to be careful who they hook up with." She smoothed her hands over his close-shorn hair. "What about security cameras?"

"Someone forgot to change a backup cartridge and the footage was recorded over."

"So no way to definitively clear your name or capture an image for the police. Dammit." Her head drooped forward onto his shoulder. "If I'd been there, you'd have a solid alibi."

"And you and your sister would probably no longer be on speaking terms. Guess which matters more to me."

"Guess which matters more to *me*?"

"We discussed this. You'll pick a time to introduce me to your dad quietly, just the two of us. We won't steal Jenny's thunder from her first official anything as Mrs. Insurance Salesman of the Year."

"Region." She smiled a little.

"Whatever." He nestled his head into the crook of her neck and inhaled her warmth and fragrance. "I won't come between you and your family."

Chapter Four

Lacey shivered in her seat on the open top deck of the bus. Dan frowned and slipped his arm around her, tucking her close against his side. The creaky vinyl upholstery and metal railings were frigid, and the cold seeped through his clothing. A brisk breeze swirled exhaust fumes up from the street and nipped at his exposed skin.

"I warned you you'd get chilled."

She glanced at him through her eyelashes and grinned. "Totally worth it." Her cheeks were as red as the wool headband and scarf he'd insisted she wear.

The view was spectacular. He just had no intention of admitting it aloud. Glowing lights traced the windows of every shop, tempting shoppers in search of the perfect holiday treasure. Angels, stars, and webs of dazzling colored lights arched over the streets, defying gravity. Crowds bundled in bulky winter clothing bottlenecked the sidewalks, gawking at the displays. Festive hats and scarves, as well as the occasional light-up novelty, brightened the sea of dark wool coats and nylon parkas. It was the perfect environment for lifting a few wallets—if one were inclined toward such things.

"The company bus covers the exact same route."

"But we'd be inside, on the lower level." She snapped another picture, then checked it on her camera. "I couldn't get these shots through the windows."

"We'd be warm." He was comfortable enough in his leather jacket, but he'd rather Lacey wasn't so exposed. Or stubborn, but there wasn't much he could do about either right now. And it was worth it to see her smile. He tucked her scarf a little closer around her neck with his free hand.

"Do you have something warm to wear over your dress tomorrow night?"

She nodded, adjusting a setting on her camera. "I've got a heavy velvet wrap. I figured it was enough to get from the car to the entrance."

He glanced at the thick layer of pewter-gray clouds. "If it starts raining, we're grabbing a cab back to the hotel."

"Spoilsport." She stuck her tongue out, and he rolled his eyes. "Anyway, it's probably too cold for rain."

"You're not helping your case, you know."

Ahead, white lights outlined the vast hulk of a department store, making it resemble a giant gingerbread castle.

"Do you want to check out the food court you mentioned? That's the store."

And I still need those candy bars for Dylan.

"Can't we come back and shop during the day? The lights are so beautiful."

Before he embarrassed himself by uttering a besotted comment about how the scenery had nothing on her, the babble of voices around them died away. Delighted "oohs" and "aahs" filled the air, and people pointed at the sky. A barrage of camera flashes added to the shimmer. It was barely more than a flurry and melted as soon as it hit the pavement, but it was snow in London at Christmas and it was enchanting.

Lacey grinned at him. "Told you it was too cold for rain."

Shimmering snowflakes dusted her hair and eyelashes. Her blue eyes sparkled with an invitation he was delighted to accept. The kiss mingled warm breath and cool lips with a trace of…peppermint? Trust Lacey to have a stash of candy canes. Maybe she'd share. Or…

He pulled her closer, basking in the heat that existed between them on so many levels, and let his hands wander. Not enough for anyone to call them out for PDA, of course. Just enough to pull away slightly, twirling a striped candy cane in his fingers.

"Hey!" Despite looking a trifle dazed from the kiss, Lacey grabbed for the treat.

"Ah-ah-ah—it's the season of giving, is it not?"

"Yeah—so give me back my candy!"

****

Lacey adjusted her earrings and studied her reflection in the dressing table mirror. The hotel stylist had achieved an artfully casual arrangement of curls and applied enough makeup to mimic a healthy glow. The sparkly ice-blue gown from her first trip to Vienna was a favorite. The sequins and plunging neckline made it a favorite of Dan's as well. It looked good, even though she suspected she'd lost weight.

But is it right for the Royal Opera House?

Dan tapped at the doorframe before entering. He hadn't done up his tie yet, and the open collar of his tuxedo shirt lent him a certain roguish appeal. His gaze kept drifting back to the cleavage showcased by her gown. He whistled under his breath. "You look amazing." He ran his warm hands down her arms and ghosted a kiss over her cheek.

She forced a smile. "Thanks. You're not so bad yourself." She twisted her hands in her lap. "Are you sure this is okay? For the ballet, I mean."

"Of course it is. I told you, there's no dress code. There'll be students in jeans and T-shirts."

"Yeah, but not in the expensive seats."

"I thought you said Mrs. Wilson bought you that dress."

"She did when we were shopping for a gown for the opera in Vienna."

"Babe, do you really think she'd buy you anything inappropriate?"

"I...no. Of course not."

Smile. Smile for crying out loud—you're upsetting him.

"Okay then. Where do you want to go for dinner?"

Her stomach gave a little flip-flop. "A restaurant, you mean?"

He frowned. "Well, yeah. There's a bunch of places on the piazza in Covent Garden. They have little heated enclosures outside so you can see the tree and shoppers. I thought you'd enjoy it."

"It does sound like fun."

Food? How many antacids can I stash in my wristlet? How far are our seats from the restrooms?

He didn't look convinced. "There's French and Japanese—"

She flinched. She couldn't help it. Dan crouched beside her chair and grabbed her hands, turning her to face him. "Hey...is your stomach still bothering you?"

"It's not so bad."

His eyes narrowed. "Bullshit. All I've seen you eat since we got here are crackers and plain spuds."

"I had some chicken yesterday."

"You swiped one tiny sliver off my plate. That's not like you." He huffed out a breath. "Well, the swiping is. The limiting yourself to one little bit? And passing up dessert? Not so much." He gentled his voice with an obvious effort. "I'm worried about you, sweetheart." He squeezed her hands, warming her cold fingers. "I want you to talk to the medic tomorrow. Please?"

"Okay."

He kissed both her hands, then stood and pulled her to her feet. "Thank you. How about a compromise? We'll stop to eat after the ballet if you're feeling up to it?"

"That would be great. But nothing too weird, okay?" She stretched up and fastened his collar. She settled his tie into place and knotted it, loving the feel of the rich silk-satin slipping through her fingers.

He lifted his chin and his lips twisted into one of his familiar smirks. "There's an American burger joint."

She smiled and kept her voice light. "I think I'm in love." She smoothed a hand down the length of his tie, reveling in the warm, solid feel of him.

He stared at her for a long moment, and when he spoke, his tone was devoid of all snark and innuendo. He rarely used that tone and when he did, she listened.

"I know I am."

Chapter Five

Dan kept his eyes fixed on the screen, ignoring the murmur of voices from the sitting room. Whatever Lacey and the company medic were discussing was her business. Health was something they'd never sat down and talked about. If this was more than an extended fling—and it was to him—maybe they needed to.

Assuming, of course, he still had a legitimate future to offer her. Henry Wilson hadn't answered his emails lately. Granted, it was the holidays and Mrs. Wilson was very active in charity circles. The old man probably got sucked into her projects.

His and Lacey's travel vouchers were approved for their next tour, but the silence was…troubling, considering the timing.

You could just cut and run. Fade into the holiday crowds and disappear.

He snorted aloud.

And prove everyone who ever said I'd never amount to anything right? Not happening.

Besides, if there was one thing he couldn't abide, it was an unfinished puzzle. And the one in front of him required his full concentration. No one had accused him of anything yet, but it was better all-around if he could solve the mystery of the robbery on the Italian tour himself and quickly.

There were six single men on the passenger manifest

from the tour, besides him. Two octogenarians—not likely candidates for "a handsome man she picked up at the pool." One of the others had hit on him in the hotel bar, so again, probably not on the list. That left three potential suspects in the tour group. Unless there was a couple working the tour.

Swell. As if there aren't enough variables.

Of course, just because the crook wore a teal wristband didn't automatically mean he was an actual Dolce Vita client. He rubbed a hand over his face and studied his own wristband. It was teal silicon, with Dolce Vita printed in discreet gold script. The bands were waterproof and relatively unobtrusive. Most guests left them on except for formal evening events.

He checked the police report again. The victim mentioned a teal wristband—nothing about the company name. She admitted to being blitzed. It could have been a plain teal wristband obtained from an event supply company or a real one lifted from a guest or employee. People lost them all the time, and the hosts carried spares.

Maybe the company should move to smart bands. Lord knows they charge enough to absorb the extra expense.

The murmur of voices from the sitting room stopped, and the front door of the suite opened and shut. He gave Lacey a moment to collect herself, then closed the laptop.

****

Lacey curled into a corner of the couch with her arms wrapped around one of the elegant crimson velvet cushions. She stared at the flames dancing merrily behind the glass fireplace doors without really seeing them. The bedroom door opened, and she drew in a quick breath.

Here we go.

Dan crossed the room on silent feet and sat down beside her. He draped one arm over the back of the sofa and angled his body toward her. "What did the medic say? You don't have to tell me if you don't want to, but— "

"You're worried. I know." Lacey hugged her pillow tighter. "He said it could be a bunch of things."

"Like?"

"Like a stomach bug or mild food poisoning. Or stress from the wedding. He asked if I'd been sticking to bottled water. And…" She swallowed hard and looked down, her hair falling over her face.

"And…?"

Her voice dropped to a whisper. "He asked if I could be pregnant."

Dan went very, very still. "Is that a possibility?"

"It shouldn't be. Jenny handles my prescriptions. I…whatever issues we've had, I trust her on this— without question. And you always use protection."

"I do. But no matter how careful we are—"

"Please do not quote a dinosaur movie at me."

He huffed out a breath. "Wasn't going to. Not intentionally, anyway."

She swallowed again, praying her nonexistent breakfast would stay put. "Are you mad?" she asked in a small voice.

"I…I don't know." He scrubbed a hand over his head. "If I am, it's not at you."

She spit out a mirthless little sound. "Who else are you gonna be mad at?"

"The universe, maybe? But not you. Never you." He relaxed with a visible effort and pried the pillow from her hands. "I suppose the first step is to find out for sure."

She nodded. "And...I mean...we don't have to...if you don't want..."

Hell, I don't even know if I want...

"Hey." He wrapped his arms around her, pulling her close. "I'm not mad at you, babe, okay? I'm just...this isn't something I've thought about. You surprised me. As for any...decisions...it's your body. It's your call. Whatever you decide, I'm a hundred percent behind you."

"It's too early to take a test. He said if the symptoms get worse, I should go to a walk-in clinic." She plastered on a shaky smile. "It could still just be a bad case of Sister of the Bride."

Dan shifted her closer, combing his fingers through her hair. "You never did tell me what was so awful about the wedding."

"You saw the pictures."

"I did. You looked lovely."

She snorted.

"I'm biased. To me, you'll always be the most beautiful woman in any room." He dug out his phone and selected a shot she'd sent him. "What's wrong with this?"

She wrinkled her nose at the short-sleeved, calf-length swirl of chiffon. "It's peach. And it's...it looks like a Mother of the Bride dress. And I had no say in the matter."

He kissed her temple. "It's you. It's gorgeous."

"I'm not stupid. I wouldn't have worn a micro mini for a wedding in a cathedral. I picked something with the least bit of style and Jenny vetoed it without even looking."

"Is that why you were so worried about being appropriate for the theater?"

She nodded against his shirtfront. "I know I screwed up—a lot—but I've been trying so hard to do better, and it felt like everything I did was wrong. I showed her the pictures I took on our trips and she blew me off. She said Dad spoiled me with the camera and the travel and 'letting me run off with some guy.' God, if I have to tell her and Dad—"

"We," he corrected. "If *we* have to tell them."

Her eyes welled up and she blinked furiously.

A kid. Do I even like kids? Does he?

"Look, I don't pretend to understand the dynamics of your relationship with Jenny…Dylan might have some insights. But as long as I've known you, everything you've done has been about starting over and doing better. If Jenny can't see that, then that's on her." He tightened his arms around her and nestled his chin into her hair. "As for your pictures, Mr. Wilson wants to talk to you about doing some photography for the company."

She sniffled and peeked at him. *Nope—he wasn't joking.* His expression was grave, with no hint of mockery. "Really?"

He nodded.

"The wedding photographer showed me some things and recommended a software package. He gave me a lot of good advice. Well, at least until Jenny decided I was 'being too friendly with him.' I mean, fine. We were friendly enough to talk about our boyfriends."

He gave her a little squeeze. "You don't ever need to defend yourself to me."

Lacey scrunched her eyes shut. "I'm sorry. It's just…the whole time…" *Dammit, do not cry. He's got enough on his mind.* "It was like Jenny's graduation times a zillion. People kept saying things to Dad like 'You must be so proud,' then they'd notice me and their smiles got stiff and they'd change the subject."

"That's entirely their loss."

"Nothing I did was right. I signed up for photography classes at the library, but then I 'wasn't being supportive enough.' "

Dan kissed her hair, then rested his chin on top of her head. "And?"

Lacey heaved a sigh. "And there was a bunch of family who never bothered with us before Dad's money and some of our mom's people I hadn't seen since we were little. It was such a load of bullshit—putting on a show for people I couldn't care less about. At least Dad'll only have to go through it once."

Dan's voice went carefully neutral. "Oh?"

"All those people stood by and watched Dad struggle to raise two girls by himself. I'm not even talking about money. Just…stuff, you know? Like saving him from the episode with the growing up book or the super fun trip down the hygiene aisle."

"Been there, done that."

"With Dylan?"

"Yeah. A very kind saleslady rescued us in the store."

"I'm just saying—those people stood by and ignored us when we needed help, so if I ever get married, I'm not throwing them a fancy-ass party I wouldn't even enjoy."

"Well, that's certainly enough to give anyone indigestion. But you know what? The wedding is over—

you don't have to worry about it anymore. And all those annoying people are on the far side of the Atlantic."

A faint smile tugged at her lips. "They are, aren't they?"

"Mm-hm." He cuddled her closer. "We're here, we're together and whatever comes our way…we'll figure it out."

"Even if there might be three of us?"

"Even if."

****

There were children everywhere. How had she never noticed before? They ran the gamut from the darling baby girl in the hotel lobby that morning trying to figure out what combination of hands, feet, and elbows equaled crawling to the rampaging hellions who'd just shoved past her on the rink. Angelic smiles, snotty noses, sticky fingers, and temper tantrums—she'd noticed more kids in the last twenty-four hours than in the last couple years of her life.

Dan's hands were steady on her waist. "Okay?"

"Yeah. Come on." She pushed away from the wall, wobbly on her rental skates. She hadn't skated in ages, and it probably showed, but it felt glorious.

Lights and carnival music filled the park, punctuated by shrieks from folks on the thrill rides. There were swings and coasters and—

Dan tracked her gaze and tugged on her hand. "Maybe not today, okay? Take it slow, just this once?"

She made a pouty face but couldn't hold it. "Okay. Just this once."

"We could check out the midway games. Maybe I'll win you a prize."

"Or maybe I'll win one for you."

A tiny boy swamped in an enormous puffy snowsuit plowed past, clinging for dear life to one of those absurd penguins. What would it be like to see all this through a kid's eyes?

Stop it. You don't even know yet.

Scrumptious food scents filled the air—coffee, hot chocolate, grilled burgers, and fried chicken. And something sweet—churros, maybe? Her mouth watered.

"I'm hungry."

Wow. I don't even remember the last time I actually wanted food.

A wide, relieved grin blossomed on Dan's face. "Great. We'll eat as soon as the session ends." He grabbed her other hand and twirled her around. She spun into him and kissed him, much to the disgust of the roving pack of teen boys.

"What you said the other night—"

"I meant it."

"Me, too." And she leaned in for another kiss.

****

The observation wheel commanded a stunning view of the park. It also made for a nice private refuge above the noise and jostle of the crowds. Lacey nestled into Dan's side and sipped her hot chocolate.

"Are you warm enough?"

She nodded and leaned her head against his chest, the warmth of the hot beverage seeping through her.

"Do you need anything before we leave tomorrow? I have to get chocolate bars for Dylan."

"From here? I mean, we're going to Germany and the Netherlands."

He chuckled, the sound reverberating pleasantly under her cheek. "It was a very specific request.

Although I'm sure she'll have no objections to receiving a variety."

"I suppose I have to get something for Jenny eventually. I just have no clue what."

And I probably shouldn't do it while I'm mad at her. Which means she'll be getting this year's Christmas gift in a decade or so.

"And your dad?"

"Yeah. He actually likes kitschy touristy stuff. Maybe a collection of souvenir T-shirts?"

"Ooh…I bet if we put our heads together, we can find some truly awful ones. Maybe language puns or something."

She giggled. "Yeah…he'd get a kick out of that."

Dan pressed his lips to her hair. "And what about you? What do you want for Christmas?"

What do I want? Everything I want is right here in this tiny compartment.

"You. Just you."

Chapter Six

Dan shifted in his seat, trying to relieve the pins and needles in his arm without disturbing Lacey. She was fast asleep, cuddling his arm like a teddy bear. She slept peacefully for most of the flight—somewhat miraculous, considering the increasing rowdiness of the other passengers. It gave him far too much time alone with his thoughts.

A kid. A job, a plus-one, and now maybe a kid. What next, a white picket fence?

He had no reference for any of this, and the old instinct to run reared its ugly head. Schiphol was one of the busiest airports in the world. He could disappear into a crowd and book a flight for…where? Where could he run where Henry Wilson couldn't track him? Not to mention Detective Devere?

Lacey stirred and mumbled something incoherent. He held his breath and she curled closer against his shoulder. Who was he kidding? He could no more leave her than he could cut off the arm she was wrapped around. And if there was a kid…and she wanted to have it…no way would he abandon his child to the kind of life he and Dylan had endured.

He blinked against the sudden brightening of the cabin lights.

No help for it now.

He stroked her cheek with his free hand. "Lacey."

She grumbled something unintelligible, and his lips curved involuntarily. The image of a little girl with bright blue eyes and messy blonde hair danced in his mind's eye. Although, he'd make damn sure to teach his kid to pick their socks up off the floor. And maybe even hang up their towels.

"Babe, you need to wake up now."

A bit of undignified snuffling, then—"Are we there yet?"

His lips quirked into a grin. "Almost. Come on—sit up. How're you feeling?"

"Grumpy. It's the middle of the damn night." She squinted in the bright fluorescence as overhead announcements began.

"Yeah…the airports are insane around the holidays, so the company books flights at off times."

Glancing around at the sea of soccer swag, he wasn't sure how successful that gambit had been. Across the cabin, another First-Class passenger picked a fight with a flight attendant about "just one more drink, sweetheart." Their seats were too far away for her response to be audible, but from her expression, she might have been offering a hot date with local constabulary when they touched down.

"How did you sleep through all this nonsense?"

Lacey rubbed her eyes. "Antihistamine. Seemed like a good idea at the time."

A burst of raucous laughter carried through the curtain dividing First Class from Coach. "You might be on to something."

****

Silent Night, my ass.

Instead of waiting calmly with Lacey while the

45

Dolce Vita staff wrangled guests and luggage with their usual efficiency, he escorted a bruised and bleeding host to the first aid station while security chased down the overbeveraged bozos who'd made off with the company pennant. The other host stood on a chair, corralling members of the group. It was not an image Henry Wilson would approve of.

Dan had gone his entire life without caring much about soccer one way or another. Now? It ranked alongside taxes and alarm clocks. Way too many people crowded the concourse, even at this ungodly hour. Ugly Christmas sweaters and reindeer antler headbands abounded, as did two distinct types of soccer swag. Sweatshirts and beanies were one thing, but cheap plastic beads, streaks of greasepaint, and team names plastered across questionable body parts pushed the boundaries of good taste. Or any taste, really. And that was just the men.

"Something going on around here?" he asked the battered tour host.

"Championship football match. Got money on it."

"Spiffy." He shot the man a sidewise look. "And I'll just forget you mentioned that."

The host shrugged and swiped a smear of blood off his forehead. "It's legal here."

They arrived at an office marked with a white cross on a green background. "You okay from here?"

The host nodded.

"Make sure you fill out a report."

"I will. *Dank je*."

Dan nodded in response. Food stalls emitted intriguing sweet and savory aromas. He purchased a bag of the local version of beignets and sampled one. Fried dough with powdered sugar. Those should tempt Lacey.

****

Lacey popped the last *oliebollen* into her mouth and licked sugar from her lips.

Dan chuckled. "Next time, I'll get a bigger bag."

Her cheeks blushed a bright healthy pink. "Sorry."

"Don't be. At least you ate something."

The motorcoach wended its way through picturesque neighborhoods topped with gabled roofs and crisscrossed by arching bridges. Water reflected twinkling holiday lights and the warm golden glow from windows.

"Do you think we'll have trouble getting into our room? I don't want to have to hang out in the lobby until after breakfast."

Dan covered her hand with his own. "We should be fine. Our arrival was scheduled around the overnight flight, and it wasn't late or anything."

"Good." She tilted her hand and interlaced their fingers. "I'm fine. Really. I think a decent night's rest and a leisurely breakfast and then we can get back on track."

He gave her hand a little shake. "Hey. This is not a race."

"I know, but I messed up London for you—"

"You did no such thing."

She leaned forward in her seat, straining to see out the window. "Is that where we're staying?"

A fantasy castle in red brick rose from the side of the canal. Turrets and gables crowned the roof and a boardwalk with café seating overlooked the canal. Elegant white stone cornices and molding picked out the windows and roofline. It promised the sort of old-world charm and excellent service he'd come to expect from the hotels Dolce Vita patronized.

The illusion lasted until they walked into the lobby. In contrast to the warm, professional welcomes they were accustomed to, the staff here looked decidedly pissed off.

The soccer-gear-clad guests milling the lobby just looked pissed.

A wreath behind the front desk hung askew, and a length of elegantly trimmed greenery was unhooked and dragging on the carpet. A small Christmas tree decorated in gold and plum baubles that matched the lobby lay on the floor beside a plinth piled high with takeout boxes. Grim-faced employees filled bins with trash and empty cans. Off-key singing echoed from the lobby bar.

The Dolce Vita guests clumped together around one of the gracious marble columns that lined the lobby. A small army of bellhops with loaded luggage carts surrounded them, like a wagon train circling up for the night. One of the ladies took a hesitant step toward a round settee, then flinched back, aghast, at muddy boot prints on the plum velvet upholstery.

The remaining hostess whispered urgently to the desk clerk. Dan sidled closer to hear and pulled Lacey along with him. A couple of the soused idiots were eyeing her. While she was normally capable of putting them in their place, he wasn't in the mood for nonsense right now.

The sound of shattering glass resonated across the lobby. Three male staff members dropped what they were doing and sprinted in the direction of one of the restaurants.

Dan slid his company ID across the counter. "Can

we get police or security to deal with this?"

The desk clerk winced. "Unfortunately, *meneer*, the police are occupied with a disturbance at the train station and securing the stadium. It will be a while before they can get here."

"So unless someone's bleeding or the building's on fire, we're pretty low on the list?"

"I'm afraid so."

"What about in-house security?"

"They are going floor by floor, but there is only so much they can do."

Dan exchanged a commiserating look with the tour hostess. "Look, I don't mean to be 'that guy,' but this isn't the sort of experience we expect."

"Of course, *meneer*. It is not the sort of experience we like to deliver."

"How long will this nonsense last?"

"The game is tomorrow—" She glanced over her shoulder at the clock. "Excuse me—tonight, and most of them will be leaving the morning after."

"So another twenty-four hours of this?" He glanced over his shoulder at the cluster of Dolce Vita guests, huddled together in their designer clothes, no doubt composing unsatisfactory comment cards. "Are our rooms at least separate from this crowd?"

"We did our best to separate fans of the opposing teams and keep them all away from our other guests, but it was not always possible."

"And I don't suppose there's any place else we could go right now for a quiet night?"

"No, sir. This is the last block of rooms in the city."

Dan offered the hostess a one-shouldered shrug. She huffed out a breath and shook her head. *Well, it's not like she has to sleep here.*

"I guess we're staying."

The desk clerk slumped with relief, then immediately straightened. "Of course, *meneer*. And we will be issuing your group room service vouchers so they can dine in the comfort of their suites."

He fixed her with a calm, level look as something somewhere shattered against the floor.

"And the general manager will be in touch to arrange additional recompense," she added, looking a bit desperate.

"Let me guess—that'll be Monday morning?"

****

The hotel interior was more contemporary than the exterior promised but still charming and elegant. Well, except for the piles of trash left outside a few of the rooms and the unattended kids rampaging in the hallway. A ball bounced off their door, rattling it in the frame.

And that explains how the decorations in the lobby got so trashed.

Their room opened into a sitting area decorated in shades of cream and plum with gold accents. A tiny tree trimmed in sparkly gold ribbons, like the ones in the lobby, but intact, sat in the center of the coffee table.

The bed was up a couple of steps, surrounded by a low wrought iron fence. Dan opened the closet and saw the small safe, which he knew better than to trust. He hung up both their garment bags.

He'd lived out of luggage—of one sort or another—for most of his life. Of course, now it was his choice. He traveled—and lived—light. All his worldly possessions fit into one large suitcase, a garment bag, and a carry-on. Lacey seemed content with their lifestyle, and of course she had the option to store things at her dad's condo. But babies needed stuff—lots and lots of stuff. And there would come a point in the pregnancy when she wouldn't be allowed to fly anymore. Would he have to stop traveling and put down roots? Now, when he'd finally gotten a legitimate chance? Resentment flared and he clenched his hand around the edge of the closet door until his knuckles turned white.

"This is pretty, but I miss the fireplace."

Dan glanced over his shoulder.

Lacey tossed her short wool coat on a chair by the door and kicked her boots beneath it. She wriggled her toes in the deep plum carpet.

He loved her—it was as simple, and as complex as that. If anyone could figure this out, they could. His face relaxed into a smile and he unclenched his fingers. "One little upgrade and you're spoiled for life."

"I'm sorry we couldn't enjoy it more."

"Stop it. You didn't do anything wrong—you got sick. It happens."

"But—"

Okay—enough is enough.

He padded down the steps and took her arm, swinging her around to face him. "Lacey, will you please stop acting like you're about to be sent into exile?" He gentled his tone and rubbed her arms soothingly. "This isn't a Gothic tragedy. You're not being packed off in disgrace because you got pregnant. Which by the way, we still don't know if that's even the case."

Her lower lip trembled, and she caught it in her teeth, stilling the motion. "This isn't what you signed up for."

"Maybe it's what I want. The two of us, partners or

51

plus-ones or whatever the hell you want to call it, as long as it's us."

"But your job…"

He cupped her face in his hand, stroking his thumb over her cheek. "Babe, do you honestly think the Wilsons would have any objections? They adore you."

"What about a home and school?"

"Home is what we make it. Plenty of people travel with little kids. Homeschooling is a thing. How about travel schooling? Think of showing our kid the world firsthand." He stopped and shook his head. *Our kid. Holy shit. How is this even a thought, much less a topic of discussion?* "And even if you are pregnant, school is half a decade away, so can you please just slow down? Whatever's going on, we'll figure it out."

She slumped her head against his shoulder. "Okay." She snaked her warm arms around his waist with a little sigh, holding on like he was her lifeline.

He tucked a hand under her chin and nudged her face up. "Now, how are you feeling?"

"Pretty good, I think." She winced as footsteps thundered past their door, accompanied by the sound of a bouncing ball. "Jeez, what time is it, anyway?"

"Much too late for this sort of crap. How about we use our lovely room service vouchers? Maybe get a plate of *poffertjes*? They're sort of like silver dollar pancakes."

"I like that idea."

"Hot chocolate?"

"Mmmm…yes. With whipped cream. Lots and lots of whipped cream."

And if that turns into kissing whipped cream off her mouth, well, who am I to argue?

Chapter Seven

Well, at least it's not my stomach this time.

Lacey pulled a pillow over her head to block out the sounds of housekeeping carts rattling past their room and the droning hum of vacuum cleaners. It was a losing battle. She'd worked enough retail and service jobs that she certainly didn't begrudge the staff a bit of banging and slamming. This wasn't a crappy chain motel. The staff obviously took great pride in their work, and the blatant disrespect for their beautiful building had to sting.

Still…it had been an awfully nice dream. It was fading, but she recollected a small boy with a gap-toothed grin and a zoo. Granted, there probably wasn't a zoo in the world that let kids play with the snow leopards, but it was a sweet mental picture.

But am I ready? There's an awful lot of squalling and dirty diapers along with the cute stuff. And how would we travel?

Dad would never toss her out—no matter how badly she screwed up. God knew she'd already given him plenty of reasons.

The trust fund is in my name. I could just disappear. No. I can't do that to him. Or Dan.

She reached out a hand and encountered empty space. The sheets outside her little nest felt cool beneath her fingers.

Unless it's already too late.

Then the edge of the mattress dipped and Dan lifted her pillow away.

"Hey—no hiding your gorgeous face." He leaned over and kissed her.

"Hmm…yeah, right." She blinked at him. "You're up…is it early…or late?"

"Here, give me that." He slid her watch off. "You're an hour behind." He adjusted the watch, then replaced it on her wrist. He brushed a kiss to her knuckles, then twined their fingers. "How're you feeling?"

"Pretty good."

"It's around lunch time. I ordered ham and more— "

"Puff…poff…baby pancakes?" Her mouth watered. Those were yummy, and the ham sounded good, too.

He chuckled and lifted her somewhat upright. "Baby pancakes."

"Why are you up and about? We got in so late."

"I slept for a few hours." He rubbed her back and she arched against his hands like a contented kitten. "I checked with local police and hotel management. Evidently, folks are very serious about their soccer here. Pretty much any public place will be swamped with drunks, and the slightest thing can set off a fistfight. The hotel is hosting a private reception for Dolce Vita guests in one of their lounges tonight."

"Wow. That's a lot of work on such short notice."

He shrugged, still tracing idle patterns on her back with his hand. "They don't want to lose the account. Besides, it gives them an excuse to keep one part of the building intact. They figure our clientele are much less likely to trash the place."

"And?"

I can see the wheels turning, you know.

"And I can see how well the hosts check wristbands. I can also cruise the room and get an idea if there are any potential troublemakers in the group."

"I can help."

His eyes narrowed. "How?"

"Bait."

"No."

"You don't think I'd make a tempting target?" She huffed and crossed her arms.

"I think the only one you get to tempt is me."

"But we're supposed to be in this together."

Come on...let me prove I'm not a liability to this...us...whatever it is we have.

"And we will be. You'll be my dazzling distraction, so no one realizes I'm working the room."

"That doesn't seem very helpful."

"Who's going to notice me when they can look at you?"

She rolled her eyes and shoved her hair behind her ears. "Before the party, do you think we can call Dylan?"

"Sure, if you want. I expect you've got girl talk to catch up on."

"No, I mean both of us. I just...I think we need a neutral third party, and she went to school for this sort of stuff."

****

Dylan looked from one to the other and heaved a very put-upon sigh. "There is not enough caffeine in the world to deal with the two of you. You know that, right?"

"But you love us anyway," Dan replied, smirking at the screen.

"Yeah, I do." Dylan took a slug of her coffee. "Your

medic probably has a checklist of things he's supposed to mention. You realize you both latched on to the most extreme possibility and let it run away with you, right?" She pointed to him. "Without sharing any gory details— thank you *very* much—you always use protection?"

He nodded.

"Okay. Cover your ears." She raised an eyebrow and gave him a look until he complied. "Lacey, you've had the same prescription for a while? You follow the directions and you're comfortable with the way it works?"

"Yes and yes."

"So you know when you should be getting your period?"

A tight nod.

"And you know what other symptoms to look for?"

Another nod, stronger this time.

"You don't look convinced."

"I know I have options. I just wish I had a better source of information than my sister." She raked her fingers through her hair. "Okay, not better, necessarily. She's a doctor. But less…"

"Judgmental?"

Lacey nodded.

Dylan pursed her lips. "I'm not a medical doctor, but I can get you reliable information, and if you want, I can set up a confidential online consultation. I'll help you any way I can."

"Thanks."

"You're welcome." Dylan crooked her finger at Dan and he dropped his hands and leaned forward.

"Okay, the first thing I want to point out is there's an excellent chance you've both gotten worked up over nothing."

They exchanged sheepish glances.

She raised her hand. "It's not impossible—if you have sex, a baby is always a possibility. I'm just saying you've taken reasonable precautions, so it's unlikely. I don't think either of you is horrified by the idea, so what's eating you?"

Lacey looked down at her hands, then up at Dan, who gave a tiny nod of encouragement before focusing on the screen. "I just came from my perfect sister's perfect wedding. If I call home and say I'm pregnant without being married and before Jenny, I will never hear the end of it."

Dylan winced. "Fair enough. But Lacey, you're an adult. You're not obligated to tell anyone—including you, big brother—more of your business than you're comfortable with."

"I know." Lacey twisted her hands in her lap until he took them gently in his own, rubbing his thumbs over her cold fingers. "It's just if I'm pregnant—"

"And it's still *if*," Dylan reminded her.

"I love my dad. I can't imagine keeping something this big from him. And I think he'd adore being a grandpa."

"But even if you ask him to be discreet, at some point he'll tell someone about the blessed event and then you're up to your ears in unsolicited comments. I get it. And I'll remind you again—you're an adult. This isn't about what your dad wants, it's about what you want."

She focused her stormy blue eyes on Dan. "And you—I get what's eating you. It's the same stuff I worry about whenever anyone gets too close. Just the fact you worry if you'd be a good parent is huge." She raised her mug, then frowned—evidently it was empty.

Dan snickered.

Dylan leveled a glare at him. "My advice is to take this one day at a time. It's too early to know if you're expecting, you're in a wonderful place, and it's Christmas. Maybe just let go and enjoy yourselves until you know there's actually something to worry about?"

Dan and Lacey exchanged another guilty glance.

Dylan sank her head into her hands, her soot-black curls tumbling around her face. "Oh, my God. What? What else could you two possibly have gotten yourselves into?"

"Not us, sis. Me. There was a robbery on the last tour."

Dylan peeked through her fingers, then straightened and tossed her curls back from her face. "Danny, statistically speaking—and by the way, I aced statistics—there must have been robberies on tours you were on before."

"But not when I was responsible for security. And not when the owner knew about me and my past."

"Was there anything you could have done to prevent it?"

"I…no, I don't think so."

"Are you doing everything you can to make sure it doesn't happen again?"

"Yes."

"And you understand there's police and hotel security and lots of other people whose job this is, who still can't prevent everything. You get that, right?"

Lacey poked him in the arm and Dylan smirked. She glanced into her empty mug again, then back at the screen.

"Look, I know the holidays have their own particular variety of baggage, but you're visiting all these amazing places. Go sing a carol or ride in a one-horse open sleigh or something, okay? And you owe me more chocolate for this. You've both got those fancy watches now, you'd think one of you could figure out the time difference."

"Sorry," they chorused.

Dylan rolled her eyes. "Seriously, though…if and when the time is right, I think you'll be great parents. And I'd love to be an auntie."

"Thanks, sis."

Lacey bumped her head against his arm. "Really…thank you."

****

Lacey perched in a high-backed chair at the polished bar and sipped her ginger ale from a delicate crystal champagne flute. She had a small plate of *bitterballen* and a sampling of local cheese, though she'd drawn a hard and fast line at the split pea soup shooters. She was eating with no apparent repercussions. That was all he needed to know.

The Dolce Vita party filled the entire lounge. The waitstaff kept the food and beverages flowing, delighted to be dealing with their usual clientele. Elegantly casual guests chatted, their voices a genteel buzz over the Christmas carols being played on a baby grand in the center of the room.

Dan draped his arm across the back of her chair and murmured in her ear. "Tell me what you see."

"One camera over the bar. It's probably set to monitor the register and make sure there's no funny business with the drinks."

He pressed his lips to her neck and felt her pulse jump slightly at the contact. "But?"

"But we could be visible."

He played with a lock of her hair. "But if we are, all anyone will see is a happy couple enjoying the party."

"I bet you wish I'd packed my sparkly little club dress now."

"I do not." He eyed her slouchy silver sweater. "The sweater blends in. The dress most definitely would not."

"So we're invisible."

"More or less." He snitched a piece of cheese from her plate. "What about exits?"

She swatted his hand. "The big double doors open on the lobby. There's a bunch of exits and elevators, but also security guards and cameras covering the doors."

Dan snorted. Security hadn't impressed him much. "What else?"

"The door behind the bar leads to a kitchen, which has to have at least one other way out in case of fire."

He pressed a kiss to her temple. "Very good."

"What'd I miss?"

"A few things. Think about the layout of the first floor. What's next to us?"

She frowned in concentration, then raised her glass to her mouth to cover it.

Good girl.

"There's a breakfast café next to us and an open coffee bar around the corner opposite the front desk."

He nodded.

"They're all small, so they probably connect to the same kitchen. So there's at least two other routes out of here, into different sections of the first floor, with access to multiple street exits."

"Excellent. You're a quick study."

"I have a good teacher. And I can handle myself."

"Lacey."

She leaned back in her chair with a satisfied smirk. "I haven't worked out in weeks. I could go check out the fitness center."

"No. Not without me."

She frowned at him. "The caveman thing is only cute for a few seconds. Then it gets old."

"Do you know what the Wilsons would do to me if I let you dangle yourself as bait?"

The frown deepened into a scowl. "You don't 'let' me do anything. I'm entirely capable—"

"I know you are. I also know you've spent the last couple of weeks subsidizing the antacid industry." His expression softened. "Babe, I'd never forgive myself if anything happened to you. Plus your father would probably murder me."

"I want to help."

"I know you do. Help by staying with me so I know you're safe. Please."

She smiled as if he'd just said something terribly amusing. "Do you see any likely suspects in here?"

"Not really." He scanned the room in the gilt-framed mirror behind the bar. "I think most of the group is either too old or too married. What about you?"

"You mean, do I see anyone I'd want to hook up with?" She smirked. "Well, there is one."

He glanced at the reflection again. None of the men in the room looked particularly enticing. He leaned in close again, a flirty smile on his face. "Which one?"

Lacey tried to maintain her smirk, but her eyes twinkled, and a giggle bubbled up from her lips. "You.

How could I possibly notice anyone else with you in the room?"

Chapter Eight

A blaring alarm and flashing strobe light jolted Lacey out of a sound sleep. "Are you freakin' *kidding* me?"

Dan flung aside the sheets and thick plum-colored comforter and got to his feet, slapping at the light switch.

She winced against the sudden flood of bright light.

"Can't take the chance. Pants and shoes." He followed his own advice, moving too quickly for her to admire her favorite scenery.

She rolled out of bed and grabbed the leggings she'd tossed on a chair after the party.

Dan lobbed a pair of socks at her. "I'm going to check the door."

She nodded—the alarm was too loud to speak without yelling—and shimmied into her pants. She shoved her feet into her socks and sneakers and pelted down the steps to the sitting area.

"The door's cool and I don't smell smoke." Dan zipped his leather jacket, then held her coat while she jammed her arms inside. "Button up—I'm not sure how cold it is outside."

She nodded and dealt with the buttons while he shoved phones and laptops into a bag. She snatched her own bag from the couch. "Wallet and passport?"

He patted his chest over the concealed pocket. "Let's go." He double-checked the door, then opened it cautiously and looked both ways.

"Fire exit's to the right, at the end of the hall."

He nodded and grabbed her hand. She pulled him close and pressed a fierce kiss to his lips. Maybe it was wacky hormones or just too many disaster movies but… *Say it—just in case it's not a false alarm. Say it.* "Love you."

His expression twisted—the soft smile he reserved for her and Dylan warring with the harsh lines etched around his eyes and mouth—and squeezed her hand. "Love you too. Don't let go." He pulled the door shut, rattled the handle once, then turned right toward the stairs.

Chaos reigned in the corridor. Guests in pajamas and robes—and less—shouted questions over the alarm, ignoring the employees directing them to the exits.

"Is there really a fire?"

"I don't want to go outside."

A housekeeper struggled to make her voice heard over the cacophony. "Ladies and gentlemen, you need to evacuate the building at once. Please take the stairs located at the end of the corridor."

"Stairs? I'm not taking the stairs."

A burly man in boxers opened his door. "Turn off that noise! I am trying to sleep in here!"

"Sir, only the fire department can silence the alarm. Please get dressed and exit the building."

The man swore in a language Lacey didn't understand and slammed his door. The housekeeper called out something in Dutch, which the crowd in the hall continued to ignore.

A silver-haired woman she vaguely recognized from the party caught her sleeve.

"Do you really think we have to go outside?"

"Um, yeah. It's a fire alarm."

"But I don't see any fire." She clutched her fluffy pink robe shut with a diamond-bedecked hand.

Dan kept walking, mouth set in a grim line. "And you don't want to. Put on your coat and shoes and grab your purse and go downstairs. Or don't. It's all the same to me." He tugged Lacey's hand, towing her toward the exit. He shoved open the heavy steel door and they traded the elegantly paneled and carpeted hallway for the bare echoing cavern of the fire stairs. They clattered down six flights of stairs, then joined the growing crowd of guests outside on the boardwalk. Sirens converged from all over the city.

A biting breeze swept over the water, chilling the sweat from their rush down the stairs. She shivered and Dan tucked her snug against his side.

"You okay?"

She cuddled closer, pulling on her gloves. "Fine. You were a bit harsh to that woman, don't you think?"

He tugged her over to one of the benches overlooking the canal. It was probably cushioned in nice weather, but tonight the bare wood sent a chill right through her legs.

"No. If a grown adult doesn't know a fire alarm when she hears one, it's not my problem. My priority was getting you and me out of there. Mission accomplished."

His words were selfish and greedy and his tone was stubborn. It wasn't a combination she had any hope of arguing against, and honestly, she didn't want to. If it was a choice between Dan and their maybe-baby or a stranger, she knew which way she'd choose—every single time.

A housekeeper and a desk clerk circulated through the crowd, the former handing out blankets and the latter checking names against a list.

"Any idea what's going on?" Lacey asked.

"We are not sure, *mevrouw*. Security was breaking up a fight on the eighth floor." She glanced at a clump of rowdy soccer fans who were belting out a song, although the end result sounded like a family of raccoons squabbling over the contents of a dumpster. "We suspect someone pulled an alarm as a distraction."

"But the fire department still has to check. Got it."

Well, there are worse places to be than curled up with the man of my dreams.

"If you'll excuse me, we'll let you know when it's safe to go inside."

Dan tucked the blanket around her shoulders, then wrapped both arms around her. He rested his chin on top of her head.

"What about you?"

"I've got a nice warm plus-one."

"It's gorgeous here. I mean, I'd really rather not be outside in my pajamas in the middle of the night, but still…" She nodded toward the row of gabled and step-roofed houses on the opposite side of the canal. "It's like a big gingerbread town."

He chuckled and kissed the top of her head. "Trust you and your sweet tooth to come up with that simile."

Her insides twinged and she shifted on the cold bench. *Stupid stomach.* "How long do you think we'll be out here?"

"Depends on how long it takes to figure out where the alarm came from and if it's legitimate."

"Have I ever mentioned I really, *really* hate soccer?"

"I couldn't agree more."

****

Lacey made a beeline for the bathroom as soon as they returned to their room. The shower ran long enough that he considered joining her. But no—she'd let him know when she was ready for a little adult recreation. He wasn't a Neanderthal and she was worth waiting for.

Besides, he had a report to finish. He didn't envy the hotel staff. Aside from actual damage, police reports, and a multitude of complaints, they still had to clean up and prepare for the next day's batch of guests. He shook his head. There wasn't enough money in the world to deal with that nonsense.

The bathroom door opened and Lacey padded out in a clean nightshirt and fuzzy socks. Damp golden hair tangled around her shoulders. "Has it finally quieted down?" She curled up in a corner of the couch.

He groaned and rubbed his hands over his face. "The fire department left. I'm not sure if the police are still arresting people."

"How bad was it?"

"Fistfight on the eighth floor, and yes, someone pulled an alarm for a distraction."

"Why'd we have to stay outside so long?"

"Because there was still an alarm showing for one of the suites. Someone dropped a butt on the carpet and it smoldered. God bless industrial strength flame retardant."

"So you mean the building really was on fire?"

"Small scale, but yeah."

"We should have a bingo card."

He set his computer on the coffee table and shifted

to face her. "Look, I don't mean to be in your business, but—"

"No, the water was not running to mask me being sick. It was running because I was freezing and needed to warm up."

He slid over beside her. "I can help with that." He tugged her into his lap and kissed the top of her head, images from too many disaster movies flickering through his head. He shook his head slightly to dispel them. She was warm and soft and safe in his arms. "So, you're really okay? And you have an idea of when you'll…know?"

She shot him a look.

"What? I can read lips. Dylan knows that."

"Yeah, I should know in a day or so." She wound her arms around his neck. "Can whatever you're working on wait until morning?"

"It is morning."

"You know what I mean."

"Yeah, it can wait."

"Then let's try and get some sleep." She slipped off his lap and tugged him toward the bed.

Chapter Nine

Lacey woke, warm and content in a blessedly silent room. The split-level design insulated the sleeping area from light from the windows and noise from the corridor. Dan's heartbeat thrummed steadily under her cheek and his arms lay secure across her back. His breath ruffled her hair slightly.

Good...he's resting.

This was what she'd been missing. She'd missed the snark and flirting and sex—hey, she wasn't dead. But this—just being with him, bodies tangled together, cuddled into soft pillows and blankets—this is what she'd been craving. Not getting up every couple of hours in search of crackers or medication to settle her stomach didn't hurt either.

Dan's breathing altered and he tightened his arms around her. "Hey."

"Hey, yourself."

He tipped his head to one side, listening intently. "Do I detect the dulcet sounds of no soccer fans?"

"I think you do."

"How're you feeling?" He shifted one hand and stroked her hair.

"I'm good. Did you get some decent sleep?"

"I did. You?"

"Yeah. Best I've slept in a while. I'm glad we talked to Dylan. I think she's right about a lot of things." She felt, rather than heard, Dan's brief snort of laughter.

"Don't tell her—I'll never live it down."

"I think anytime people try to make a perfect anything, they just drive themselves crazy. But like she said, we're in this amazing place at Christmas and I think we should just go with the flow—go see the things and eat the sweets, and whatever doesn't work out this time, well, there's always the next trip and the one after that."

"Good. I won't even make fun of what you eat."

"This works both ways, you know. You're coming with me. You're not spending the entire trip in here writing reports. You're going to let go and let the police and security people do their jobs." She extended one hand with the pinkie crooked. "Deal?"

He linked their fingers and pressed a kiss to her hair. "Deal."

He smoothed his hands down her back, over her candy cane print nightshirt. She had something—okay several somethings—more alluring in her luggage, but her body needed a few days to get with the program.

Dammit.

Still, he shouldn't have to wait. Her hand drifted south, but Dan caught it.

"It's no fun if I can't reciprocate." He lifted her hand to his mouth and kissed it. "Partners, remember?"

"But you—"

"I don't want sex." She raised an eyebrow and he chuckled. "Okay, I don't want *just* sex. That's not what this is about, remember? I want *you*—happy, and healthy, and…" He glanced down through his lashes, "…fully satisfied."

"Pretty sure of yourself, Mr. Lewis."

"Damn right."

"Do you know what day it is?"

"Monday…I think?"

"No, besides that."

"Since you're the one with the guidebook, I suspect you're going to tell me."

She propped herself on one elbow. "It's the night before St. Nicholas Day."

Dan shifted himself into a sitting position against the headboard, pulling her along with him. She straddled his lap and draped her arms over his shoulders.

"I think I see where this is heading."

"I think we need to go exploring and find *Sinterklaas* and Black Pete and eat all the chocolate and see all the lights and—"

"And you think we can do everything in one day?" He planted a kiss on her forehead.

She leaned up and kissed him lightly on the lips, morning breath be damned. "We can certainly try."

"As plans go, I've heard worse. And maybe we can find some fun street food? You have to leave some chocolate for the kids, you know."

She nodded. "If we must."

"You haven't lived 'til you try the brined herring."

"Blech." She wrinkled her nose. "I've seen videos online. I am not fighting a seagull for a dead fishy."

"*Appelflappen*, maybe?"

"Apples? That sounds yummy."

"*Hagelslag?*"

Her eyes narrowed. "Now you're just making things up."

He shot her a wounded look. "Why would I invent something you can verify online in thirty seconds?" He grabbed a phone from the nightstand and passed it to her.

"Here. I'll wait."

Dubious, she opened a browser. "Hagel—"

"—slag."

She typed in the rest of the word and hit enter. "Whoa. Seriously? Bread with chocolate sprinkles? Yes, please."

"Just make sure you get chocolate and not drop."

"Which is?"

"Licorice."

"Blech."

"And as I recall, you've got a new dress in need of a spectacular event to show it off."

"I do."

"Our last night here there's a wine and cheese cruise on the canals, followed by the Dutch National Ballet's *Sleeping Beauty*. It's Tchaikovsky, with spectacular costumes, like *The Nutcracker*. There's even a cat."

"Sold. What else?"

"I'd like to go for a walk around the red-light district and make sure the notes in the brochure are up to date."

"What did we just talk about? I'm coming with. I wanna see if I can spot stuff out in the real world."

"It's not a competition."

"No, it isn't. We're partners—you watch my back, and I watch yours. Besides, doesn't the brochure say not to wander around questionable neighborhoods alone?"

"I've got a particular shop I want to visit."

"I want to go to a cat café."

"Um…you do know the words café and coffee shop don't always mean actual coffee here, right?"

She fixed him with a wide-eyed, vapid stare. "You mean they might serve…illicit substances?" She snickered. "I'm well aware."

****

The Christmas market was awash in the scents of cinnamon and ginger, as well as the mouth-watering aroma of sizzling sausages. Happy shoppers thronged the stalls, singing along to the brass band playing "O Tannenbaum." Evidently, security was tight enough to prevent any soccer-fan-related destruction here, although they'd passed a few shops with broken windows and mountains of trash on the streets.

"Look, babe—a skating rink." Dan turned with a firm hand on Lacey's back as he deftly moved them out of range of the punk angling just a little too close. Said punk tripped over his own feet reaching for a pocket that suddenly wasn't there anymore, then scowled and melted into the crowd. "Amateur."

"Where there's crowds, there's pickpockets, right?"

"Right." He'd never worked a scene like this, no matter how desperate he was. Drunks in the red-light district were fair game, but this place was full of happy families. He went his entire childhood without being brought to a place like this. No way in hell would he take that away from another kid.

Lacey squeezed his arm. "You wanna give security a description? Or let him take his chances?"

"I doubt they'd even bother writing it down in this kind of crowd."

But what if the creep is out for more than easy wallets? What if he hurts someone? Jeez...I've read too many comics.

"Dan?"

He released a long slow breath and relaxed his shoulders. "It's Christmas. He gets a pass."

This time.

She twined both hands around his arm, keeping her bag between them. "Can we go skating? And get hotdogs and one of those waffle cookies?" Her eyes sparkled and she vibrated with excitement.

"And another terrible T-shirt for your dad?" He glanced around the laughing, chattering crowd. Shoppers milled the stalls, and kids shrieked excitedly, their cheeks stung red by the cold. *So many kids…*

The band struck up a tune that lilted like a nursery rhyme and the crowd—especially the children—sang along enthusiastically. The song tugged at his memory, though the only word he recognized was *Sinterklaas*.

"Why do I feel like I've heard this before?" Lacey wondered.

"I expect you have."

She canted her head, a question painted in her expression.

"Your dad and his old movies. A little girl sings this song in an old black-and-white classic about Santa Claus. You probably saw it every year when you were growing up."

A little crinkle appeared between her eyes.

"Oh, come on, New York City girl—I bet you even went to the store the movie's set in."

Her eyes widened and she clutched his arm. "Oh my God, you're right! Every year—even after Jenny tried to burst the Santa Claus bubble for me."

His expression darkened. "I encouraged Dylan to believe for as long as I could."

She wrapped both hands around his arm and squeezed. "Of course you did." She pressed up on her toes and kissed his cheek. "You're a good brother."

"I tried."

"You succeeded."

He shook his head slightly to banish the past. "Where do we find jolly old St. Nick?"

"He's not Santa, exactly. He doesn't have reindeer and elves. His helpers are these dudes dressed like they're going to a ren faire."

"No red suit or ho-ho-ho?"

"Nope. *Sinterklaas*—St. Nicholas—looks sort of like an old-time bishop."

His mouth ticked up in a half smile-half smirk and he looked over her shoulder. "You mean like that guy?"

Lacey whirled around. A saintly, white-bearded old gent wearing a tall, pointed hat and carrying a staff smiled benevolently. One of the soot-faced fellows bowed over an out-stretched leg and Lacey handed him her camera. He snapped a couple of shots, then bowed and returned it.

She checked the images before tucking the camera away. "I don't even remember the last time I had a picture with Santa. Dad's gonna flip."

Dan slung an arm around her shoulders. "Good."

"What about you?"

He kept his tone light. "This is my first time."

Lacey stopped and looked at him, stricken.

He gave her a little squeeze. "Hey…it's fine. This is way better than a random photo of a scrawny kid with a crappy mall Santa."

"When we get to Germany, they have this sort of Christmas angel. You need to get a picture with her, too."

"Nah. I've got my own, and she's way prettier."

Her cheeks flushed pink. "Flatterer."

He kissed her temple. "It's not flattery—just plain truth."

"But seriously—if we—if I'm—"

He stopped and set his hands on her shoulders, grounding them both. "If you're pregnant, our kid is gonna meet all the Santas and angels and—I dunno—Easter bunnies? All the stuff me and Dylan didn't get— "

"Our kid will be loved, is what you mean. And…you mean it? 'Our kid?' "

"Well, yeah."

"It's just…you said you'd support my decision. You never said you wanted—"

He swallowed a hard lump of the past. "It's a lot to think about, you know? I never really considered…but yeah. If I helped make a kid, and you wanna have that kid…I'm not going anywhere." He leaned down and kissed her—right there in the middle of the market. Her strong, warm arms twined around his neck, holding him firmly in place. After a moment there was a scattering of applause accompanied by a chorus of "oohs." They broke the kiss to more applause and quite a few camera flashes. Heat crept up his neck. *Dammit.* He rested his forehead on Lacey's. "They must think I just—"

"There are worse things. Just go with it." She smiled at the crowd and waggled her left hand, even though she was wearing her red wool gloves.

More applause and a few calls of "*Gefeliciteerd.*" A chubby-cheeked baker in a green-striped apron bustled out from her stall and presented them with two heart-shaped ginger cookies.

It was entirely more attention than he was comfortable with, but Lacey glowed with happiness, and that made it worthwhile.

It made a lot of things worthwhile.

Even picking up her socks off the rug every morning.

****

Lacey wandered down to the sitting area in her socks and stooped to press a kiss to the side of his head. He leaned into her warmth, still focused on his screen. She grabbed his mug and took a long sip.

He reclaimed it and swallowed the dregs. "Want me to order more from room service?"

"I'm good."

"What're your thoughts on renting a couple of bikes and riding around to see decorations tomorrow?"

She sank into the corner of the sofa, tucking her feet up and pulling a cushion into her lap. "Maybe in a couple of days? Just not tomorrow."

He looked up sharply.

Is she pale? Or is it just her green sweater combined with not-so-flattering lighting?

"No—it's fine. I'm not…well. I'm…not pregnant."

"How—?" The penny dropped. "Oh. Are you okay? Can I get you anything? Chocolate? A heating pad?"

"A hug?"

"Always." He slid over beside her and wrapped his arms around her. "At least we know."

"Yeah."

"Is this a good thing?"

"Probably. I mean, I'm glad you don't hate the idea, but I don't think I'm ready right now, and I think we should have a plan before we invite little Plus Two along for the ride."

He pulled back enough to fix her with a wide-eyed look. "You? A plan? I guess I am a good influence."

She made a grumpy little noise, then nestled against his chest. "The best."

"If only I could influence you to hang up your

clothes."

She rolled her eyes, and he chuckled.

"For the record, I don't think we're ready, either, but we would have made it work."

"I know." She wrapped her hands around his arm.

"You're sure you're okay? I mean, aside from…?"

"I'm a big girl. I've been dealing with this for a few years now."

"Yeah, but you're my girl, and I worry."

"I think it was just wedding stress plus 'the medic said what' plus—"

"—stress. I get it. Just please…the next time anything remotely like this happens, please just tell me."

She tipped her head up and met his gaze. "I will if you will. Partners, remember?" She eyed his computer. "Are you ready to stop working and come to bed?"

"Go get comfortable. I'll be right there." He held his smile in place until she disappeared into the bathroom. Then he got up and checked the window and door. He switched off the lights, and the image of the little girl in his mind giggled, then ran off down the path. His eyes stung. *Maybe someday…*

Chapter Ten

Lacey pulled her cranberry wool sweater over her head and smiled at her reflection. Her cheeks flushed a healthy pink without makeup. *What do you know—being an ocean away from constant criticism is good for my health. Okay, probably eating actual food instead of a steady diet of antacids helped too.*

Behind her, Dan folded the heather-purple sweater she'd worn yesterday and placed it in a drawer.

"Could you toss me a pair of socks?"

"I can do better than that. Merry Early Christmas."

He handed her a glossy silver gift bag that rustled enticingly when she squished it. She pulled out a couple layers of glittery tissue paper and offered him a crooked little grin.

"You got me socks for our super romantic first Christmas together?"

He rolled his eyes. "Yes, because you complained your toes were cold and I'm a thoughtful guy."

"Yeah, you are." She leaned up and kissed him, then turned her attention to the contents of the bag. So many vibrant colors! Stripes, snowflakes, trees—

"Cats!" She rubbed one against her cheek. "They're so soft!" She sat down and pulled on the woolen cat socks over her leggings, then laced her boots. She admired the results in the full-length mirror, grinning at the cat faces peeking over the top of her hiking boots. "I love them. Thank you."

"Only the best for you. Now, I know I can't talk you out of coming with me—"

"Nope."

"Taking pictures is frowned upon, so make sure your camera is secured."

Her grin turned impish. " 'Cuz that'd be such a fun email—'Look where we went today, Dad.' "

"So what's the first rule of walking around a dicey neighborhood?"

"Keep my eyes moving and my hand on my bag."

"Close." He stepped over in front of her chair and engulfed her small hands in his and tugged her to her feet. "How about take my hand and don't let go?"

"I can manage that."

****

"Wow. This is very…um…"

"Wow?" Dan suggested, sniggering.

"Yeah." She was hardly a nun, and she'd visited colorful neighborhoods, especially since she started traveling abroad but this was so…blatant. Maybe even worse than Montmartre. Scantily clad prostitutes posed in windows lined with red neon. The smell of weed tickled her throat. It was just so odd to stroll the cobbled street alongside the canal and see boobs outlined in fuchsia neon on the façade of a gracious old red brick building.

Wow, indeed.

Dan offered one of his patented one-shouldered shrugs. "I think we could learn something from the way they do things here. They figure people are gonna people, so they just regulate enough to keep things safe. They save their efforts for the dangerous stuff."

"I think this would give most of Dolce Vita's clientele a collective conniption."

Dan smirked and tucked her hand a little tighter into the crook of his arm. "I think you're right, but remember other tours come here at different times of the year. Some of them attract younger people looking to sample the local nightlife." He glanced around the neighborhood with an expression of faint distaste. "Some of these bars are supposed to be fun."

"I think even old me would give this a pass. Although—" A hint of speculation crept into her voice.

"No. We will not look for a postcard to send to your sister." He steered her out of the path of a car trundling down the narrow pavement. The driver honked at a cyclist, who raised one hand in a fairly universal gesture.

"Spoilsport." They stepped around a bike rack and continued on their way. "Have you seen enough for your report?"

"I have."

"So we can go to the cat museum now?" She bounced on her toes.

He caught her around the waist and swung her over a pile of dog poo before she stepped in it. "Sure. Just one stop along the way."

****

"Oh my God…I cannot believe that was an entire shop full of condoms."

My face must be the color of a fire hydrant.

Dan, of course, looked perfectly cool and collected. "And yet I couldn't help but notice you made a purchase."

"So did you!"

"They carry products from all over the world. I have

81

fond memories of a brand I purchased in Vienna." He gave her a lascivious once-over with a hint of a smirk playing over his lips. "Gotta be well stocked for when you're feeling better."

She rested her cheek against his arm. "Soon, I promise."

A crowd consisting of tourists, locals, and a couple of stray cats gathered around a food cart on the corner. She couldn't understand the languages spoken, but it looked like dares or maybe bets were taking place concerning the consumption of small dead fishies.

Yuck.

"Sure I can't tempt you?"

She indulged in a full-body shudder. "Nope."

A teenage girl held a herring by the tail for her friends to take pictures. She shrieked as a gull swooped in and snatched it.

"Make that a double nope."

Boats glided past on the canal with barely a swish of water marking their passage. The crooked narrow old streets boasted more bikes than cars. And—

"Is that a parking lot…for bicycles?" She'd never seen so many bikes in one place, neat rows of them in a fenced-in corral. Most sported large serviceable baskets.

"Yup. Bikes are a big thing here. Cyclists managed to delay the renovations on the Rijksmuseum with arguments about the bike path that cuts through the property. We still have time to rent a couple if you want." He guided her around a corner, dodging across the bike lane.

She glanced at her phone and frowned. "I thought the cat museum was another two streets that way?"

"It is, but there's a good flower market here. Maybe

you'll find a present for Jenny."

"Like a really prickly cactus? Or maybe a Venus flytrap?"

Dan snickered. "I think you'd have trouble getting those through customs. I thought more along the lines of a pretty bauble for her tree."

"I like my idea better."

He opened the door, and a breath of warm, humid air gusted out. She ducked under his arm into a shop awash in color and scent. Buckets of cut flowers in every imaginable hue circled the tables and displays. Bunches of dried flowers and herbs hung from the ceiling. Open crates of bulbs lured shoppers with the promise of spring.

Lacey elbowed Dan. "See? Cactuses. Look at those spines."

He caught her elbow and turned her slightly. "Look—tasteful Christmas baubles."

"Ooh…what about a pair of those tacky wooden shoes?" Another display caught her eye. "Or the smelliest cheese we can find?"

"What about staying on speaking terms with your sister so I can meet her someday?"

****

Lacey stretched like a contented cat and relaxed against the sofa cushions. Her feet rested in Dan's lap and his long clever fingers massaged away pressure points from her boots. She sniffed the red rose he'd bought her and closed her eyes.

"Did we buy enough chocolate for Dylan?"

He snickered. "There's no such thing. But I'm sure we can get more in Nuremberg. I'll have the hotel ship our parcels in the morning."

She yawned, covering her mouth with the back of

one hand. " 'Scuse me. I should email Dad and let him know about the box the store is shipping for me."

"I imagine he'll figure out for himself that the bottle opener with the wooden shoe for a handle is for him."

"And the ornaments are for Jenny. Well, if she hates them, she can always hang them on the side facing the wall."

Dan squeezed her feet. "I can't imagine hating anything my sister chose for me."

She snorted. "You haven't met Jenny."

****

Lacey smiled at her reflection. A couple days of lazy mornings, good meals, and strolls through fresh air had her excitedly anticipating this evening. She'd made up whatever weight she'd lost from the steady diet of crackers and antacids, and the snug sleeveless satin bodice of her new dress hugged her curves perfectly. The deep V-neck revealed enough cleavage to catch Dan's eye while still being respectable enough for the canal cruise and ballet.

Dan zipped her dress, then slid his palms over the sleek midnight-blue satin. She shivered delightfully beneath his hands, even as she secured her hair with one last pin. He tugged her closer, and his buttons pressed into the bare skin revealed by the low-cut back of her dress.

"You look amazing." He bent his head and planted a kiss on her shoulder, then one on the side of her neck, taking advantage of the skin bared by her elegant French twist. "And this dress is giving me ideas."

She turned and touched a finger to his lips. "Patience. I didn't go to all this trouble to get ready, just to have this dress land on the floor before we even leave the room."

"Are we planning on some…dessert after the ballet?" He ran his hands up and down her spine, leaving trails of goosebumps on her bare skin.

"We are."

Dan took hold of her hand and spun her. The skirt's asymmetrical hem had an edge of deep black lace that flared around her. Laughing, she twirled back against him.

"What're those?" Dan jerked his chin in the direction of the well-appointed bed, where she'd set two matching gift boxes.

"Early Christmas presents."

"Do we really have to go to the ballet tonight?"

"Hey, you're the one who arranged everything." She smoothed a hand over his pristine white vest, then adjusted his glossy black silk-satin tie. "Besides, I don't get that many opportunities to ogle you in the tux."

He caught her hands and kissed them. "You can ogle me any time and any place you like, Miss Devere."

"I might just take you up on that. *After* the ballet."

****

Lacey studied her appearance in the mirror, recollecting the evening. The candlelight cruise through beautifully decorated neighborhoods was charming. Bare tree branches outlined with twinkling fairy lights stretched toward the sky, casting a golden glow over the streets. Lights edging the storybook buildings were reflected in the swirling waters of the canals. Fantastical shapes wrought in lights hovered over the water, part of an annual art display. The wines she'd sampled cast a lazy glow on the evening.

The ballet was an enchanting fairy tale come to life.

The glittering royal court costumes were astonishing, but the cheeky cat was her favorite. *And how on earth did the ballerina do all those spins on one foot?* She'd been the recipient of any number of looks ranging from appreciative to envious. Dan had taken advantage of every moment of seclusion to kiss her.

"You're not working out there, are you?" she called through the bathroom door.

A guilty pause, followed by some muffled shuffling sounds. "No. Of course not. You're not leaving towels all over the place in there, are you?"

"Um, nope." She stooped and grabbed two off the floor, shaking them out and flipping them over the shower curtain rod. "Did I get the right size?"

"You did. I love the feel of silk against my skin."

She grinned at her reflection. "You may have mentioned that."

The blue silk negligee clung in all the right ways. She ran a brush through her hair, fluffing out the golden curls over her shoulders. She checked her breath against her hand. Anticipation built in her veins like fizzy champagne bubbles, and a rosy flush spread over her fair skin.

Stop fussing. You've done this before. He knows…well, everything.

Show time.

She switched off the bathroom lights and paused in the doorway, eyeing her lover. The deep blue silk suited him. He sensed her presence and looked up. A slow smile curved his lips. He offered her a tiny stemmed glass filled halfway with a brown liqueur.

"What's this?"

"Something local. I think you'll like it."

She sniffed rich notes of chocolate and mint, then took a sip. It burned pleasantly all the way down to her stomach. "Ooh…I bet this would be amazing on ice cream."

"Are you sure you want to get so…messy?"

She took another sip, then set her glass aside. She selected a truffle from a box on the bedside table and fed it to him, shivering pleasantly as his lips caressed her fingertips. "Not messy. Disheveled, maybe?" She savored a chocolate of her own as she shrugged out of her robe and draped it over his on the chair. Then she slipped into his lap and ran her hands across his chest.

She felt his warmth and strength easily through the layer of thin silk. "Do you like your present?"

He finished his drink and set the glass aside. His hands glided over her body as he nuzzled her neck. "Very much so. I especially like the bow." He slid one hand along her bodice and caressed her through the delicate material.

"I thought you might."

He hadn't fastened the buttons of his pajama top, making it a simple matter for her to push it off his shoulders. He pressed a kiss behind her ear. "So…can I unwrap my gift?"

"If you don't, we're going to have words."

She felt him grin against her neck. He untied the dainty satin bow and loosened the lacing with a delicate fingertip. The straps slid down her shoulders and revealed the upper swell of her breasts. "So beautiful…" He kissed down her throat and chest to the edge of the silk, then loosened the ribbon a bit more. The silk slipped farther down. She wriggled her arms out of the straps and Dan reverently pushed the delicate cloth to her waist, replacing it with his hands and lips. He pressed soft kisses between her breasts, and she felt his warm breath against her skin. His calloused fingertips rasped against her soft skin, but his touch was unfailingly gentle.

She stood and allowed the gown to slide down and pool at her feet. Dan took advantage of the change in perspective to close his warm mouth around her nipple. A small, incoherent sound escaped her lips. She ran her hands through his close-cropped hair and held his head right where she wanted it. He slid his clever hands to her hips and pushed the scrap of gossamer fabric down.

She laughed and tugged him to his feet. "You have me at a disadvantage." She returned the favor, undoing the drawstring of his pajama pants and gliding her hands inside.

He cradled her face in his hands and kissed her deeply.

She kept trying to push the pants down his hips. He smirked against her mouth, his face crinkling with laughter.

After a moment, he nudged her gently toward the bed. "Why don't you get comfortable?" He slipped his pants off and revealed the toned body that never failed to take her breath away.

But even with his amazing physical attributes on display, it was his fathoms-deep blue eyes that held her gaze. He might argue that he didn't have the words to express his feelings, but she knew. He told her with every touch, every glance. They might not be ready for little Plus Two yet, but when they were, that child would be cherished, just as she was.

She propped herself on her elbows and watched as he selected a foil packet from the top drawer of the nightstand. "Fresh from that very interesting store?"

He glanced over his shoulder. "Indeed." He turned back, condom in place. "Are you sure you're okay?"

She pouted and shook her hair back over her shoulders, letting him get a good long look at just how sure she was. Then she stretched out one leg and tried to hook it around him.

He chuckled and caught her ankle. He rested one knee on the bed and stroked his fingers up the inside of her leg, then pressed a kiss to her knee and another to the inside of her thigh. A hint of five o'clock shadow tickled very sensitive skin. She giggled, and Dan smirked. He leaned over her, keeping his weight on one elbow. She arched up and kissed him, and he slid home.

Pleasure sparked along her nerves as he moved inside her. "Love you," she gasped against his lips.

****

Home. That's what this was. Him and Lacey, moving together. Wherever they were, if they were together, they were home. He loved her for her whole self, but oh, how he'd missed this connection. Being embraced in her warmth was exquisite. She wrapped her legs around his waist, as if to hold him in place—not that he had any intention of going anywhere. It had been so long since Italy, and he wanted to make this last, but Lacey of course had other ideas. She wound her arms around his shoulders, pulling him impossibly closer.

Her mouth tasted like chocolate and peppermint and he laughed against her lips.

"What's so funny?" she gasped between kisses.

"You and your sweet tooth." He kissed her again, reveling in the sugary richness on his tongue.

She twisted slightly and nipped at his ear and he was

lost. His last bit of restraint evaporated and he tensed his fingers in her soft skin. Her body clenched impossibly tight around his and he shuddered his own release. After a moment, he rolled to the side, careful to keep his weight off of her. He bowed his head for a long moment, catching his breath. "Give me a minute?"

She nodded with a blissed-out smile.

He kissed her temple, then slid from the bed, heading for the bathroom. He attended to the condom, then splashed cool water on his face and hands.

"Do you need anything?"

"Just you."

He slipped back into the bed and drew the soft cotton sheet up to their waists. "Well, you've got me." He traced one hand lightly from her cheek, down her neck, and over her collarbone to cup her breast. He stroked his thumb lazily over her nipple. "Are you—?"

She glared at him. "Seriously? After that, you're asking if I'm—"

He leaned over and dropped a light kiss to her pouting mouth. "Actually, I was going to ask if you were hiding any more of those chocolates over there since the taste is so amazing second-hand." His hand drifted beneath the sheet to rest on her stomach.

"Ask me nicely."

His hand slipped lower, gentling her through her own waves of pleasure.

"Keep—ooh—doing that and you can have the whole box."

Chapter Eleven

The flight from Amsterdam to Nuremberg was flawlessly efficient and unaccompanied by high-altitude barfing or partying. The transfer to the hotel and check-in were orchestrated with the level of care and comfort Lacey expected from Dolce Vita. Of course, it was too good to last.

Lacey rattled the door handle. She turned it one way, then the other. No dice. The bolt still stuck out, preventing the door from shutting. She tried shoving it in with the heel of her hand. "Ow! Crap." She shook out her hand. "Dan, come look at this door, would you?"

"What is it?"

"It's stuck with the bolt thingy out—it won't shut."

"Well, this connecting door won't lock at all, so we're not staying here."

She sank onto the funky modern sofa—totally at odds with the antique architectural details of the room—and leaned her head against the back...or tried to. Instead, she sort of slid down the oddly oval-shaped cushions. She stared at the ceiling with its dainty plaster scrolls and flowers. "This is three out of three, isn't it?"

He nodded, dialing the phone. "Hello? This is Mr. Lewis—no, everything is not to our satisfaction. Neither of the doors in this room locks. We need to be transferred immediately."

Lacey stuffed her feet into her boots, half listening

to Dan's conversation. This hotel featured an eclectic mixture of bold, modern furniture and accessories in a grand old baroque building. Massive olive settees sported stiff oval cushions that looked like they escaped from the set of a sci-fi movie. An assortment of cream-colored legless "chairs"—like upholstered sand chairs—completed the furnishings.

Who the heck wants to sit like that anywhere but the beach? And what if you're wearing nice clothes?

A weird conglomeration of clear glass globes sprouted from the ceiling—someone's idea of a chandelier? Whatever the designer's intent, the effect was jarring next to the delicate plasterwork—not to mention downright un-sit-down-able. And she just wanted to get settled in and maybe have a nap to make up for a serious lack of sleep the night before. While lack of sleep due to sexy fun times with Dan was infinitely more satisfying than disruptions due to delayed flights and missed transfers, it was still lack of sleep. Their flight was too short to do more than doze.

Seriously, though—three out of three? Was this trip cursed?

"Look, I'm the executive security consultant for Dolce Vita. I report directly to the owners. Do you really want me to—thank you. We'll be waiting." He moved their bags to the door and took a quick look through the bedroom and bath while she scanned the sitting area.

He draped their jackets over the bags and eyed one of the low, legless chairs, then shook his head, leaning against the wall instead.

Lacey dug her heels into the carpet so she wouldn't slide completely off the sofa. "Do you think Mr. Wilson would consider 'butt ugly' a good enough reason to take this place off the list?"

"No, but the fact that he wouldn't be able to sit in those chairs might do it."

She winced, picturing the older folks in their group. The comment cards would be brutal.

****

Lacey completed a circuit of their new room and rejoined Dan in the sitting area. "No connecting door, the windows don't open, and all of the mirrors are on interior walls. The fire exit is four doors to the left."

Dan leaned down and kissed her forehead. "Good job. And you know—the door locks."

She eyed the weirdly shaped olive and cream furniture. "If only there was a comfortable place to sit." A Christmas "tree" made of bare wooden sticks displaying a scant selection of neutral-colored baubles occupied the center of a low table. "I don't get it. It's such a pretty building, why didn't they go with nice old-fashioned-looking stuff to match?"

"Well, the exterior's baroque. That style furniture is massive and ornate. Whole rooms full of it can get a bit overpowering."

"Okay, but there has to be a compromise between incredibly overdone antiques and whatever the hell this is supposed to be."

Dan peeled his gray wool sweater over his head. As always, she enjoyed watching the play of his muscles when he moved, and the way his shirt came untucked. He noticed her eyeing him and his lips curled in a slow smirk.

Which she reciprocated. "What? Can't a girl admire the scenery?"

"Only if I can return the favor. Are you

comfortable? I wanna turn down the thermostat a couple of degrees."

"It is a bit warm. I thought it was just because we're dressed for outside." She pulled off her own sweater and tossed it on a chair.

"Ahem. Remind me again what's the easiest step you can take to prevent hotel robberies?"

She rolled her eyes and recited: "Experts suggest keeping your hotel room tidy is one of the best ways to deter potential theft. A thief is less likely to choose a neat room where any disturbance will be immediately obvious." She grabbed her sweater and lobbed it at him.

He caught it and draped it over his arm, heading into the bedroom.

"Does the bed at least look comfortable?"

"Yeah, but I think I'm going to take off the comforter. Are you sure the windows don't open? Not even a crack?"

"Nope." She perched gingerly on the sofa and pulled off her socks, dropping them on the rug. "What's the best time to shop at the Christmas market? I wanna see it all lit up, but I need a gift for Jenny and maybe something else for Dad, and I expect it's jammed at night."

"You know they probably won't get there on time, even with expedited shipping. And...I don't really know."

"But haven't you been on this tour before?"

The shuffling sounds from the bedroom ceased.

"Babe?"

"I...you know Dylan and I never had any of this holly-jolly happy families stuff when we were kids."

She kept her voice level, even though the idea of such a bleak childhood made her heart ache. "I know."

She blinked furiously to contain the tears stinging her eyes.

"Just because I never had it doesn't mean I was willing to wreck another family's happiness. I stayed far away from the traditional stuff. I'd go to museums in the day and conduct any…business…at night, usually in the club district."

"So this is your first real Christmas…ever?"

"Yes, I suppose it is."

His voice was much closer, and she looked up. He leaned against the doorframe. Bare feet, an open shirt framing nicely understated muscles, and the top button of his jeans undone.

Close your mouth. Drooling isn't at all cool.

She sauntered over and slipped her arms around his waist. She ran her hands across his back, reveling in the feel of warm skin over solid muscle beneath her palms.

Does he realize how strong he is to come through everything life threw at him and still be a fundamentally decent person? Well, if he doesn't, I'm happy to spend the rest of my life showing him.

Wait. My whole life?

She glanced up through her lashes. Dan regarded her with the soft smile he reserved for her and Dylan. His arms encircled her, telling her with his touch how much she was cherished.

Maybe? Am I ready for that? Is he?

First things first.

She stretched on her toes and kissed him. "Then we are going to make this one amazing."

And I really need to up my gift game.

****

Dan rolled over and punched the pillow.

Maybe this place has a pillow menu. I'd kill for a couple of those high-tech cooling ones right now. Goose down is just too damn hot.

Lacey had already kicked off the sheet and he'd stripped down to his boxers. The mattress dipped and creaked as she sat up. The bedside clock provided a dim glow—just enough to see her pull off her skimpy silk slip and toss it at the foot of the bed. She slumped back with a little huff.

"That's not doing anything to lower the temperature in here, you realize." He knew the dips and curves of her figure as well as his own reflection, and he grinned at the pretty mental picture.

"It's too hot to flirt," she grumbled.

"It's never too hot to flirt."

She rolled on her side facing him, and he ran a teasing hand down her side, over soft warm skin, until his sensitive fingers encountered the lace band of her panties. He rubbed his thumb over her hipbone. He'd never not want her, but…damn, it was December in Germany. How were they so sweaty before they'd even gotten started? "Do you want a cool drink?"

She shook her head. "I think that would wake me up too much. I want to get some sleep, so we can go to the market. We have to get a picture of you and the Christmas angel."

He leaned in and brushed his lips against hers—just the barest hint of a kiss. "Told you—I've already got my own." As always, the feel of her lips was intoxicating, and he leaned in for one more taste. And then the thought percolating in his brain for the last few days bubbled to the surface. "Can I ask you something?"

She propped her head on one hand. "Like what?"

Deep breath. Damn, it's hot in here. And stuffy, And—

"Have you ever thought about getting married?"

"I—what?"

"Not a wedding—you've made your feelings on the subject abundantly clear. And I agree. But marriage? Just you and me, but—I dunno—formalized?"

Lacey flopped over onto her back and stared at the ceiling. "Wow. Whatever I expected—that was not it."

Well, now I'm awake.

"To be honest, it's not something I ever imagined saying until we were facing the possibility of little Plus Two."

"It's not the fifties, you know. People don't 'have to' get married just because they're expecting—which we're not."

His heart hammered against his ribs—had he just screwed up everything? "I know, but it does make some things easier legally." *Humor. Lighten this up.* "Or so I've heard. Not much of an expert on what's legal."

"I know I want to be with you. It's just…neither of us really has any context for a stable marriage. The only good one I can think of off the top of my head—"

"Is the Wilsons?"

"Yeah."

"There are worse role models. And wanting to be together is a good starting place."

She huffed out a soft breath of laughter and rolled back to face him. He brushed a lock of hair behind her ear, then traced his fingers over her face.

"D'you think we'd ever end up like them?"

"Fabulously wealthy?"

She scrunched her nose. "Again, there are worse

things. But traveling the world and still together after how many years?"

"Enough that their daughter should have been about your age."

"Maybe a bit older. Her name was Penny. She was adorable."

"I can't imagine pain of that magnitude, but they worked through it. And they still look at one another like there's no one else in the world." He twirled one of her curls around his finger. "I never really thought in terms of forever, but what they have…that could be nice."

She shifted closer on her pillow. "Okay. Honestly, my dad is a little concerned that I'm so far away, and you can't legally speak for me in an emergency. So there's that." She caught his hand and laced their fingers together. "But…I dunno…that seems more like a business arrangement than a marriage. Are you… Dan, are you proposing?"

"I…I don't know? I don't think so. Yet." *Oh, that's smooth.* "This is all so new."

She squeezed his hand and held it so he could feel her heartbeat—and some very interesting real estate.

"It's new to me too, you know. I think we should take a little time to get used to what we have right now before we add any additional passengers or paperwork. Deal?"

"Deal." Their hands were too entangled for a pinkie swear, so he tugged her forward and tickled her instead. She giggled and rolled on top of him.

Who needs sleep, anyway?

****

Dan tossed the smoke-blue alpaca sweater on the chair near the door.

Too damn hot for wool. In Germany. In December.

Lacey perched on a low, round olive-green velvet…thing…at the dressing table—seriously, what was this hotel's issue with normal chairs? She wore a top with skinny little straps and had braided her hair up off her neck. He sauntered over and kissed her shoulder. The feel of her skin—like sun-warmed flower petals beneath his hands and lips—was one of his favorite things, but—

"You know it's only hot in here, right? There's snow on the ground outside."

She glanced over at the pile of outerwear on the end of the sofa and shuddered. "I know, but I can't bear the thought of piling all those layers on until we're ready to go. Did you call about getting the heat fixed?"

"I did. They said they'd send a maintenance guy today."

"They better. I can't handle another sweaty night." Her breath caught as she seemed to realize what she just said.

He lounged against the wall, arms crossed, and his lips curled in a sinful smirk. Her blazing cheeks and scrunchy face were adorable. Not to mention dead sexy. It was an oddly endearing combination. It was…Lacey. *Try analyzing that one, Dylan.* "Since when do you object to a little recreational…sweat?"

She shimmied into her gray leggings—and did that really require so much wriggling? Not that he was complaining, mind you. Mission accomplished, she shrugged into a plaid flannel shirt and fastened the buttons. Then she sashayed over to his bit of wall and trailed a teasing hand down his chest.

"I don't, generally, but I do like to follow it up with a nice recreational snooze. Which did not happen last night." She plucked a familiar navy-blue sweater from the pile of clothing and pulled it over her head. It hung adorably baggy on her petite frame, hitting her at midthigh.

His eyes narrowed. "You don't have enough clothes of your own? You're reduced to pilfering mine?"

"I like the color." She winked at him, coupled with a saucy grin. She turned her face into her shoulder and sniffed. "Besides, it smells nice." She collected her boots and socks, then glanced over her shoulder. "I mean, you're entirely welcome to re-pilfer it at your leisure."

He swallowed hard to clear his throat…and calm a few other bodily functions. *Did the temperature in here just go up? Again?* "You know damn well if I come over there to reclaim my sweater, we won't be leaving this room anytime soon."

"And would that be so very terrible?"

****

Entering the Nuremberg *Christkindlesmarkt* was like being shrunk down into one of those expensive toy villages people set up around the Christmas tree. Snow dusted the cobblestones and a multitude of voices babbled in more languages than he could count. Somewhere in the warren of booths, a children's choir sang an unfamiliar tune. The joy in their voices was unmistakable…if a trifle off-key. Warm, spice-laden air emanated from the candy-cane-striped pavilions.

"So we need a few more tacky souvenirs for your dad and a nice gift for Jenny?"

"Do I have to? I got her those tree ornaments in Amsterdam."

"Well, if she was my sister—"

"Yeah, but your sister isn't a—"

He laid a leather-gloved finger over her lips. "Come on—season of good fellowship and kids in the vicinity and all that jazz."

"Fine. Something nice for Jenny. And more chocolate for Dylan."

"Of course." He rolled his eyes. "And we have to find the Christmas kid since you're so set on it."

"*Christkindl.* I think she's kinda hard to miss." Lacey checked the directory and pointed to a graphic. "See? Big gold angel."

He looked over her shoulder and noted a security and first aid station on the map. CCTV cameras were mounted near the entrance to the market and the ATMs.

"Oh, and I want to see the fountain where people make wishes."

"And get a picture for your dad?"

"Well, he never objects to more pictures, but I don't think he's heard of this one. I read about it in the guidebook."

The church bells in the medieval tower overlooking the plaza tolled the hour. The crowd stopped browsing and haggling to stare at the colorful clockwork figures of a drummer and bell ringer playing their instruments. Seven little men dressed like lords or maybe princes paraded past the king seated on a throne beneath the clock face. Midday sunlight glimmered off the king's golden robes and crown. *Perfect time to lift a few wallets.* He tugged Lacey in front of him, wrapping his arms around her—and incidentally, her bag—so she could enjoy the spectacle.

Uniformed police in high-visibility vests cruised the crowd. The city obviously took the safety of their guests—and all their foreign currency—seriously. Old him would have found circumventing them a delightful challenge. New him was just as happy to watch them cart off a couple of dumbass amateurs before they ruined someone's holiday. He shook his head.

I'm getting soft.

"No, you're not."

He looked down sharply.

Wait—did I...?

Lacey met his gaze with a soft smile. "No, babe, you didn't say it out loud. I could tell by the look on your face." She hugged his arm. "You've always been a good man. You just needed the chance to show it."

****

Lacey sucked in a deep breath of crisp winter air. Her mouth watered at the scent of sizzling sausages and sugar-dusted fried dough. And gingerbread—there was definitely gingerbread happening in the vicinity. Her stomach rumbled audibly.

Dan chuckled and tugged on one of her braids. "What do you want to do first? Wishing fountain or Christmas angel?"

"Fountain maybe? I've heard it can be hard to find the ring you turn to make a wish."

"Cool. We'll go find the fountain and wish to find the angel."

She wrapped her free hand around his arm. "And then we can have sausages and mulled wine?"

"It's blueberry wine here. You might not like it."

"We can share."

"Uh-huh. That means if you like it, I'll get two sips. Maybe. If I'm lucky."

She rolled her eyes. "So then we'll get another. And there's all sorts of getting lucky, you know."

"There are indeed."

His low, smokey tone brought a rush of warmth to some wildly inappropriate places. She elbowed him, which didn't have a great deal of effect through all their layers of winter clothing. "Behave."

Another decadent chuckle. "Where's the fun in that? You want the blood sausage, right? With lots of sauerkraut?"

"Eww!"

"Pork knuckle? Pickled eggs?"

"Yuck." She swatted his arm. "I swear, you invent this stuff to gross me out. And just for that, you owe me some chocolate."

Dan pointed to something up ahead. "Is that your fountain?"

It was as if someone had transplanted a towering Gothic church spire on ground level. A collection of meticulously detailed medieval saints, knights, and lords graced the structure, which was surrounded by an elaborate wrought iron fence. The figures were painted in vivid shades of red, blue, and green, and a rich, golden yellow. A line formed behind a man holding a little girl up to turn the ring while another man snapped pictures. His husband, judging from their smiles—not to mention matching hats and scarves.

"Looks like it's not too hard to find after all. Are you sure you can reach it?"

"Well, if I can't, I'm certainly not doing *that*." She frowned as a girl wearing a beanie from a US school climbed the fence to reach the ring.

And this is why American tourists get such a bad rap.

"The sign says it's a replica. She's not climbing an

actual medieval relic."

"Don't care. I don't like when people disrespect monuments at home so I'm not doing it here."

"Fair enough."

They moved to the head of the line and stepped up to the fence. The gold ring was small—without the line of tourists, it would be hard to spot. She reached up, then balanced on her toes, barely brushing the ring with her fingertips. *Dammit. Maybe*—"Oh!"

Dan scooped her up, holding her against his chest. She looped one arm around his neck for balance and turned the ring the requisite three times, then squeezed her eyes shut and made her wish. Laughter bubbled up as he swung her around and set her on her feet. They strolled away arm in arm.

"What did you wish for?"

She glanced at the couple currently at the fence. An elderly man turned the ring while his wife held his hand. Something about them recalled the Wilsons, even if they weren't as opulently dressed. "If I tell you, it won't come true."

I wished for that to be us someday.

****

Lacey dragged Dan from one booth to the next. Nutcrackers, delicate blown glass baubles, and so much gingerbread! She could easily find enough stuff to decorate every room of a mansion in a different theme. Calliope music from the carousel warred with the tunes of a polka band and the shouts of vendors hawking their wares. A stray tabby cat scurried by with a pilfered sausage dangling from its mouth.

And then she spotted it. An entire booth filled with little people made of—yup, it said so on the sign. Stacked prunes with walnut heads.

Dan looked from her to the display warily. "Those are for your dad, right?"

"Nope."

"Lacey, they're very cute, but your sister really doesn't strike me as the folksy sort."

"Come on—can't you just picture a whole oom-pah band lined up on her mantle?"

"No, I can't. How about a nutcracker? Or one of those beautiful miniature buildings?"

She offered him a bit of side-eye, accompanied by a pouty lower lip. He leaned in and kissed the pout right off her face.

"Or we could table this discussion, go for a ride on the carousel, and maybe get Jenny something personal when we get to Vienna? Since you already sent something festive for the house."

"Do you really think I can so easily be distracted? Just by an amazing vintage carousel that looks like it's made of peppermint candy?"

"I do."

"And you'd be right."

Chapter Twelve

Dan wiped his face and straightened his shirt while the call went through. The heat had most definitely *not* been fixed while they were exploring the market. He set the towel out of range and faced the screen just as the video connected.

Mr. Wilson looked relaxed in a cheery red sweater over an open-necked plaid shirt. The room behind him was comfortably elegant with a large Christmas tree bedecked with clusters of red glass baubles, shiny tin soldiers, and red satin bows looming in the corner. A pair of nutcrackers presided over an array of framed photos on the mantel—mostly of a younger Martha Wilson, first with an infant, then a gap-toothed toddler with golden pigtails, and finally a pale waif sporting a brave smile and a pink headwrap. A heap of presents wrapped in glossy white holly-print paper and tied with wide plaid ribbon bows flowed out over the floor beneath the tree, creating a perfect holiday card. "Hello, Dan. Merry Christmas."

"And to you, sir."

"I'm sorry it took me so long to get back to you. My little retirement project seems to be eating into my time more than the position I retired from. End-of-year reports, and proposals for future tours, plus all Martha's holiday projects. I've read everything you sent me." Mr. Wilson leaned forward, studying the screen. "Why are you sweating? Have you just come from the gym?"

Damn. He resisted the urge to wipe his face on his sleeve. "No, sir. The thermostat in our room is broken." He shifted his backside on the modern whatever-the-hell-it-was he perched on and envied the older man his leather upholstered desk chair.

"Is this the same place where you had the broken door lock? Or was it rampaging soccer fans?"

"Door lock. Soccer fans was Amsterdam."

"I must say, these aren't the sort of experiences Dolce Vita is known for. You let me know what the hotel management does to make it right. I expect a nice dinner or a good bottle of wine at the very least—in addition to correcting the problem. And if they don't, well, there are other hotels in the city."

"It'll be in my report."

"And on the subject—Dan, much as I admire your dedication to your new post, I must point out—no one expects you to single-handedly solve the issue of crime in the tourism industry. Excuse me." He paused and looked over his shoulder. "Yes, Martha, I will." He turned back to his screen, mug in hand. "Martha says she hasn't heard from Lacey recently. She wants to know all about the wedding, and of course, your current holiday."

Not the damn wedding... "I'll let her know."

"Please do. I want Martha to take a break and sit for a while. We're hosting Christmas Day at the children's hospital and she's running herself ragged with the gifts and the caterers and the celebrities." He shrugged slightly. "I don't recognize any of the names, but Martha has her sources, and she assures me they're all very popular people."

"I'm sure the families will appreciate everything."

Mr. Wilson closed his eyes for a long moment, suddenly looking his age. "The holidays can be terrible in those places, and some families have other children to think of. We just want to provide a bit of hope and distraction if we can." He sighed, then straightened in his chair. "I might take her away somewhere for New Year's."

"The Dutch National Ballet has an exquisite production of *The Sleeping Beauty*. Lacey and I enjoyed it very much. I imagine she'd love that."

"She would. I think I might even stay awake through it. Now, as I was saying…your job is to help us make it a bit harder for the criminals to prey on our guests. As for Italy, well, the young lady made some ill-advised decisions, and there were consequences. I'm sorry, of course, but 'Romeos' preying on lonely female travelers is a very old phenomenon. I will consider your ideas about the wristbands though."

"Thank you, sir."

"Now, will you please relax? You've been spending far too much time brooding about Italy and sending me reports. It's Christmas. Take Lacey somewhere fun so she can tell Martha all about it."

"I will."

"You've done fine work this year. Your holiday bonus should hit your bank account any day now."

"That's very generous, sir."

Mr. Wilson waved a hand dismissively. "It's nothing you haven't earned. Have you and Lacey decided where you want to go next?"

"From here we're going on to the winter art tour through Italy and France."

"That's a good choice for this time of year. There

are blustery days when you want to be inside, but there's usually at least a few mild enough for exploring. And after that?"

"Lacey likes the architecture tour."

"Is that the one that stops in Barcelona? With those buildings that look like a kid drew them in crayon?"

"That's the one."

"Well, you've got to cover all of them eventually. Email your request to my office and they'll get started on the paperwork—*after* the holidays. If that's what Lacey wants, tell her to get lots of pictures. I'm using one of the ones she sent from London for a company-wide email. I need to get her set up for commissions." He took a sip from his mug. "We do have that upcoming project in the spring. It's a new venture, so I'd like to have you with us."

"The wedding cruise? Or should I say, The L—"

Mr. Wilson wagged a finger at the screen. "Do not let Martha hear you say that. She's entranced with the idea of pretty dresses and flowers and whatnot. I have a more…pragmatic view of the subject."

"I think men generally do."

"Indeed. Now I want you to enjoy yourselves. I don't expect to hear from you again until after the holidays unless it's a purely social call. Is that understood?"

"Yes, sir. It was…good talking to you."

Mr. Wilson leaned forward, studying his screen. "Dan, did you think I took so long getting back to you because I suspected you were involved with what happened in Italy?"

A flush crept up his neck, despite his attempts to hold his expression impassive. *Never, ever underestimate how sharp that man is.* "It did occur to me."

The old man chuckled. "Dan, I'm very fond of Lacey, but I'd never put this company at risk. Do you understand me? If I thought for an instant you'd betrayed my trust, well…you wouldn't have to wonder. You'd know."

The breath whooshed out of Dan's lungs before he could contain it. Of course, Mr. Wilson's keen eyes spotted that, too.

"My boy, what happened in Italy was obvious and clumsy. You are neither. You'd never have stayed off Interpol's radar so long otherwise. Now, I mean it this time—stop worrying at this and go enjoy yourself."

****

Lacey sat cross-legged on the bedroom floor with her laptop and rested her back against the side of the bed. Way more comfortable than any of the so-called chairs.

"You look beautiful, honey."

She blew a lock of sweaty hair out of her eyes. *Right. Of course I do, Dad.* "You look…like a blank screen."

"Eh, I don't know how all this crazy stuff works. But I can hear you, so that's good enough for me. Where are you?"

"Nuremberg, Germany."

"Nuremberg, huh? That sounds like a weird place to go for Christmas. I mean, your great-granddad was there at the end of World War Two, and some of the stories he told were pretty rough."

Lacey took a sip of her water before answering. "I know, but before the war, Nuremberg was known as the Christmas capital of Europe. They had the best toy markets and gingerbread. That's what they're trying to recapture."

Dad must have been grinning—she could hear it in his voice. "I'm so proud of you—learnin' all this new stuff. I never pictured you bein' the one to go to the ballet and opera and all those fancy places."

Gee, thanks, Dad.

"I know your sister's wedding wasn't the right time, but I wanna meet this fella of yours. I think he's really good for you."

"I know he is." She took refuge in her glass again.

"Look, I know the wedding was—"

"It was Jenny's day. I get it."

"Yeah, but some of the family…"

She thumped the glass on the carpet hard enough to slosh water over the rim. "You know what, Dad? Those people aren't my family. They made their choice twenty years ago."

"Lacey, someday I'll be gone—"

"And I will get by just fine." She flipped a braid over her shoulder.

"Yeah. I think you will. I love you. You know that, right?"

"Love you too, Daddy."

"And hey—I got the box you sent. I love those salt and pepper shakers that look like the big red buses. You really rode in one of those?"

"Yup. It even snowed."

"Huh. You never think of snow in London. Rain, maybe. And I put the magnets on the fridge. Just don't buy me any more neckties, all right?"

"But you looked so distinguished!"

"I'm not wearing another of those damn things until your wedding, young lady."

That'll be a long wait.

"Are you sure I can't send you anything?"

She smiled at the blank screen. "I'm good, Dad. Remember, anything I have with me has to go in luggage."

"Still getting used to that. How about the next time you're home we go to the camera store? I bet those fellas could find some kinda fancy whatsit for your camera."

"That sounds great. There's more stuff coming from Amsterdam, but it might not arrive in time."

"I'm not five…it doesn't have to be under the tree on the twenty-fifth. I like whatever you send me, whenever you send it."

"One of the boxes is for you and Jenny both. Everything's marked."

"I'll be on the lookout. I love the T-shirts. I don't understand what any of them say, but I love them. I'm sure Jenny'll love whatever you sent her."

"They're ornaments for her tree, so she can open them whenever they arrive."

"I bet they're pretty. She's got a schmancy interior designer doing their holiday stuff, but I'm sure—"

Lacey huffed out a mirthless laugh. "It's fine, Dad."

"Aw, baby…I just want you two to be friends again. I know you two have had—"

"Open warfare?"

"Differences. But she's your sister and she loves you."

Right. That's why she decided to dress me up like Great Gramma Rose.

"You're going to her place for Christmas, right? I don't need to worry you're home alone eating a microwave dinner?"

"Yeah. I just hope she serves real food, you know? Ham or turkey or something I can recognize. Jenny goes back and forth between that micro bionic crap or the fancy caterer who serves those tiny little bits of nothing in the middle of a big plate with a drip of sauce around the edge."

She smothered a laugh with her hand. "That's why I filled up your freezer from the gourmet meat company. You should have plenty of steaks and burgers. And it's all organic, grass-fed, yadda yadda if Jenny gives you a hard time."

"My freezer is my kingdom, and your sister can keep her nose out of it. I plan on defrosting one of them steaks, and that's what I'll make myself if I don't get enough to eat at your sister's. No TV dinners on Christmas. Cross my heart."

"Love you, Dad."

"Love you too, baby girl. Merry Christmas."

****

Lacey wandered into the sitting area intent on another cool drink from the fridge.

And we'd better not be getting billed for any of it, seeing as how it's still about a zillion degrees in here.

Dan levered himself up from the legless chair, stretching out his back. "Did you have a good call with your dad?"

"I did. He's delighted to have a new shaker for the salt Jenny doesn't want him to have on his burgers. How about you? You seem like you got something off your mind."

"How can you tell?"

She padded over and traced her fingers over his forehead. "You get a crinkle, right here. It's gone now."

"Mr. Wilson set me straight on a few things."

"Good. I'm glad."

He caught her hand and kissed it. "He asked where we want to go after the art tour. You still interested in the architecture tour?"

"That's Barcelona, right? With the really cool curvy buildings?"

"That's one way of describing them. Just remember, there's probably gonna be some medieval buildings and maybe even some super ugly modern crap."

"I don't mind the medieval ones. It's fun to try and imagine how they built them without computers and cranes and all that. And you and I are pretty good about escaping and finding our own forms of entertainment."

"And he wants us on the wedding cruise."

She winced at the word "wedding." "Well, I've never been on a cruise. And it's a big ship. There's gotta be someplace we can escape the crazy, right?"

"I dunno. An entire cruise ship full of weddings is a lot of crazy. And a cruise is, by definition, in the middle of the sea."

"Gee, thanks."

He shrugged. "Wanna check out the gym?"

"And come back to this all sweaty? No thanks." She headed behind the bar for the fridge.

He twisted to loosen up some grumpy muscles. "I haven't been in a couple weeks."

"Ooh yeah…it really shows."

He didn't reply and she paused with her hand on the fridge door and looked back. "Dan?"

He plastered on a smile. "It's not as much fun by myself."

Realization hit like a freight train and the blood

drained from her face. "You didn't go alone because you wouldn't have a solid alibi if there was another incident. Why didn't you say something?"

"Because you weren't feeling well and I didn't want to be a jerk."

She rubbed the heels of her hands over her eyes and up to her temples. "I could have come with and sat and soaked my feet. I'm sorry. I was selfish and—"

He came over and peeled her hands away from her face. "Hey. You had a lot on your plate and you weren't feeling great. I'm not accustomed to having someone around I can count on. And both of us are still getting used to the whole 'partners' thing. It's a learning curve."

"But you shouldn't always be the one making accommodations for me."

"Not a ball game—we're not keeping score."

"The luck we've had with this place, the gym is probably out of order."

"There is that." He squeezed her hands. "How about you find us some cold drinks, and I'll fill that fancy tub, and we'll have a nice cool soak?"

"I like the way you think...partner."

****

The corner spa tub, rendered in beige granite and green marble, wasn't quite big enough for the two of them, but they made it work. Dan rested his arm on one edge of the tub and Lacey's feet stuck out the far side. She'd added lavender bath salts to the water and the scent was pleasantly languorous.

A cold bottle of complimentary Riesling from room service sat on a tray table, along with a cheese plate and a selection of tiny fruit tarts. Dan drained his glass and set it on the shelf surrounding the tub. He brushed his lips against her neck, then her shoulder. "How're you feeling?"

"Better." She let her head loll against his chest. "Cooler, anyway. I didn't anticipate that being an issue in Germany at Christmas time."

"Me neither." He nuzzled her neck and toyed with the end of one of her braids. "You never did tell me what you want for Christmas."

She caught his hand and traced her fingers lightly over his. "You've already given me the world—literally—and a bag of socks. What more could a girl ask for?"

"It's our first Christmas together. I wanna do it right."

"I don't need something wrapped up with a shiny bow...and I definitely don't need to pay an overweight fee for my luggage."

"This is true. I've lifted your luggage."

"Hey!" She splashed a bit of water his way. "What about you? What did you ask the *Christkindl* for?"

"I've got you." Another kiss to the side of her neck. "I've got a spiffy silk robe." His hand wandered beneath the water, drifting along her belly. "Don't need much else."

Her breath caught in her throat. "Is that a candy cane in your pocket, or are you just happy to see me?"

His hand moved lower. "No pockets." Another kiss with a hint of five o'clock shadow tickling her skin. "And I'm always happy to see you."

"Maybe...ooh...maybe we should move this to the bedroom?"

"You have the best ideas. Next to mine, of course."

Chapter Thirteen

"Beer and a pretzel do not count as dinner."

"Says who?" Lacey took another big bite, then held it out to him.

Dan took a more decorous nibble, followed by a sip of beer. "Maybe we can acquire food containing actual protein?"

"This is just the appetizer. I want potato pancakes and more of those little sausages and—hey!"

A couple of boys breezed past, jostling her arm and sloshing beer down the front of her coat. A woman pushing a stroller hurried after them, scolding. She called something over her shoulder that Dan guessed was an apology. Her words were lost in the happy chaos of the market.

"You good?"

Lacey shook beer off her hand. "Yeah. I made it this far without making a mess. I guess I was due. The hotel has a dry cleaning service, don't they?"

"Probably. Not entirely sure I'd trust them, though, with their track record." He tracked the happy family— Mom and Dad smiling, two roughhousing preteen boys, and a happy toddler bundled up in a pink snowsuit. Dad pointed at the ATM sign and headed in that direction.

Lacey noticed where he was going. "Dan? Isn't it a weird time for the ATM to be serviced?"

His gaze snapped in the direction she was pointing.

Are you freakin' kidding me?

A team of armed men wearing jackets with *Sicherheit*—security—printed on the back was opening the ATM—in the middle of the crowded market with no police nearby. And the laughing father of three was headed right for them.

He gave Lacey a little shove toward the main part of the market. "Go—the shopkeepers all have phones and most of them speak English. Have one of them call the cops and tell them the ATM is being robbed."

"But—"

"Go!" He was already moving. No way in hell would he stand by and see a happy family shattered a few days before Christmas. He glanced back once and saw her pushing her way through the crowd, out of harm's way.

The scene in front of him unfolded in a bizarre combination of slow motion and horrifying speed. One of the "guards" turned and pointed a gun at Dad, who raised his hands in supplication. Mom shrieked and grabbed one of her boys by the hood of his jacket. Dan shoved his way in front of the family.

There was a sound like a car backfiring.

But there's no cars here?

Then a searing pain in his arm. The colorful holiday lights swam drunkenly overhead and his half of the pretzel and beer threatened to make a reappearance. The horizon tilted and he realized his head was on a level with…boots? *That can't be right.*

A woman screamed, drowning out the music and laughter of the market. Then even that dwindled down to silent darkness.

****

Disinfectant fumes stung his nose. Bright white light penetrated his eyelids. He tried to turn his head and bury it in the…pillow? Yeah, pillow. *Crappy pillow. What happened to the fluffy goose ones?* His head refused to obey him anyway.

"Dan? Can you hear me?"

Small warm fingers clenched around one of his hands. The other was numb. Everything was muzzy.

Why can't I move?

The thought sent a jolt of adrenaline through him. Not that his body had any intention of moving in the near future.

"Is he awake?"

Other voices, saying things he couldn't understand. He vaguely recalled being lifted from the ground…and barfing all over the person doing the lifting. *Oops.* Then…an ambulance? Something in need of shocks and a wheel alignment, anyway. At least whatever he lay on now wasn't moving.

"Herr Lewis?"

Mouth…feels like cotton…gotta move…

He licked his lips…or tried to.

"Dan?"

"Fräulein, if you could perhaps—"

"No."

Oh, I know that tone…

His mouth moved a few times before producing any sound. "Lacey?"

"I'm here."

The pressure on his hand increased. He wanted to squeeze back but managed only a feeble twitch.

"Herr Lewis, can you open your eyes?"

"Too bright." He swallowed thickly and screwed his

eyes shut. He heard rustling and caught a faint whiff of lavender and…beer?…then a soft hand on his forehead.

"Dan, it's me. Can you please open your eyes?"

Her hand cut the glare just enough. He blinked up at red-rimmed blue eyes in a chalk-white face.

"You're…mess…babe…"

She let out a strangled laugh. "Pot, kettle."

He shifted his eyes without moving his head. Glaring white walls, bright overhead lights, a stainless-steel counter—well, he certainly knew an emergency room when he landed in one. A brief scuffle punctuated by the squawk and static of a police radio passed by the door. "Hospital?"

"Yeah."

"Family?"

"Does he wish us to contact his family?" someone out of his line of sight asked.

"No. There was a family at the ATM. That's what you mean, isn't it?"

He nodded gingerly. *Why does my head feel like lead?* "Dad…and kids."

"They're fine—all of them. Thanks to you."

"Bad guys?"

"The cops got them. No one else was hurt."

"Fräulein, if I may?" A man in green scrubs with a stethoscope hung around his neck moved Lacey away from the bed.

Dan frowned at the newcomer.

The doctor grinned in response. "*Ja*, I know—I am not as pretty as your friend. But I need to check your reactions." He pulled out a penlight. "Please do not punch me." He shone the light in Dan's eyes. "Very good. Now follow my finger with your eyes. Just your eyes, please. Do not turn your head. Good. Would you like to sit up?"

Dan grunted, his mouth too dry for words.

The doctor was unfazed. He fiddled with the remote and the bed slowly raised Dan to a sitting position.

The room tilted oddly on its axis, then settled. He realized his jacket, shirt, and sweater had been removed. A nurse and a man in a Dolce Vita uniform gossiped in the corner, eyeing him appreciatively. Lacey hovered just behind the doctor, twisting her hands together.

"How do you feel? Do you need a basin?"

He took a minute to take stock of himself. Everything seemed to be attached. His mouth felt gunky and he swallowed again. He shook his head—then wished he hadn't.

"Perhaps some scrumptious ice chips might help?" The doctor grabbed a cup from the bedside table and held a spoon to Dan's lips.

Cool, blessed wetness flooded his tongue. He worked the chips around his mouth until they melted.

"Is that better?"

"Yeah. Thanks, doc."

"Dr. Zimmermann."

Dan frowned for a moment as the word filtered through the smattering of basic German in his mind. "You mean my sawbones is—"

Dr. Zimmermann threw back his head and laughed. "*Ja,* my name means 'carpenter.' And if you can make bad puns, you will be just fine."

Dan turned his head and frowned at the bandage on his right arm. He tried moving his fingers, and a searing bolt of pain shot through his entire arm. "What happened, exactly?"

"You have a bullet graze to your right deltoid muscle. You can thank your leather jacket that the bullet did not penetrate deeper. You have a large bandage and you will need a sling for a week or so, but there does not appear to be any permanent damage. You will have a very heroic scar. You also have a mild concussion from hitting your head on the cobblestones. Can you tell me what day it is?"

"Friday?"

He glanced at the clock on the wall. "Technically it is Saturday now. We will keep you a full twenty-four hours for observation, due to the head injury, which means if you have no complications, you will be released Sunday morning. I believe the police wish to take a statement. There is a translator here from your tour company, should you require assistance."

"And the family? They're really okay?"

"They are." He grinned. "You did good, my friend. I will send the officers in, then we will move you to your room. Merry Christmas."

Dr. Zimmermann stepped back, and Lacey immediately took his place, looking torn between fury and terror.

"You scared me."

"I'm sorry. I just…I couldn't let that man walk into an armed robbery. Not with his kids right there. I couldn't."

"I know." She sniffled and tears streaked her cheeks. "I thought you weren't a hero?"

"There's a quote from an old sci-fi show in there somewhere, isn't there?"

"If there is, I'm sure you'll tell me all about it."

"What happened? I sort of lost track after—"

"After you got shot?"

"Grazed."

"And smacked your skull on the cobblestones." She sighed. "I ran and got a merchant to call the police, like you told me. When I got back, there was a crowd and you were on the ground and—"

"I'm sorry." He slid his good arm around her and drew her head down to his shoulder. Her tears fell hot on his skin. He ran his fingers awkwardly through her hair. "I don't suppose my leather jacket survived this encounter?"

She pressed a kiss to his shoulder, then raised her face, smiling a little. "I'm afraid not. They had to cut it off to treat your arm. But I'm pretty sure Santa will bring you a new one. After all, you've been very good this year."

Chapter Fourteen

Lacey's eyes flew open. Again. She blinked in the semi-darkness, registering her surroundings. Walls and curtains in the shade of industrial barf green some genius thought was soothing, a bedside table on wheels, latex glove and hand sanitizer dispensers mounted near an overly-wide door... *Hospital room. Right. Not the morgue or the cemetery. He's fine.* Her stampeding heart didn't quite get the memo.

Dan shifted on the bed, crinkling the plastic mattress cover. *Must be what woke me.* She yawned and rearranged herself in the crappy vinyl cushioned side chair. Hospital furniture was the same the world over, and it all sucked. Her coat slipped to the floor when she moved. It stank of spilled beer, penetrating her clogged sinuses. Footsteps and the occasional rolling cart passed the door. Announcements came over the PA, mostly in German, since it was well after visiting hours. A round wall clock ticked away the minutes.

It was everything and nothing like the New York City hospital where she'd waited to see if Dad would make it. Then, the doctors directed all their communications to Jenny, which made sense because medical jargon was more obtuse than any foreign language. Now, no one spoke to her because...well, really, there was nothing to tell. Dan was *fine*—a bandage and a bump on the head. He'd be released tomorrow morning or whatever morning was twenty-four hours from now and they'd go back to bitching about the broken thermostat in their room and enjoying the trip.

But it could have been so much worse.

Tears and yesterday's mascara gummed her eyelids together. She blinked and rubbed them until her eyes focused properly. A nurse had dimmed the lights for the night, but she could see Dan clearly. Except for the bandage and the pillows propping up his arm, he could have been sleeping in their bed at the hotel. The image of him crumpled and still on the cobblestones rose in her mind and she stifled a sob. Fresh tears stung her eyes and she scrunched up her face, willing them not to fall.

"Hey…you okay, babe?"

He was awake. Of course he was. She wiped her face on her sleeve.

Ugh. Something else for the cleaners.

"I'm sorry…did I wake you? Do you need anything?"

"Just you. I don't sleep so good on my own anymore."

"Yeah…not sure how well that'll go over. We're lucky no one's kicked me out yet."

"We're a package deal. They kick you out, I'm coming with." He scanned the room, frowning. "I don't like it here."

"I know. Not enough exits. It's just for twenty-four hours."

"Closer to thirty-six," he scoffed.

"You hit your head. They need to monitor you. Look, at least the thermostat works."

He made a noncommittal noise.

"You're at the far end of the corridor—that's why you have such a lovely view."

"Which I can't see from here."

"There's a fire door directly across the hall. The nurse's station is six doors to your left, and the elevator bank is six doors past that."

"Thanks. Security cameras?"

"Seriously?" He was *so* pushing his luck.

He shifted a bit more on the bed. "At least come over here where I can see you better."

"I'm all blotchy and gross."

"You're gorgeous." He held out his good hand.

She dragged her chair across the linoleum to the side of the bed, adding a few more scuffs along the way. She laid her hand on his forehead—cool, no fever. *Thank God.* "Do you know where you are?"

His lips curled in a familiar smirk. "Hospital in Nuremberg because I'm a dumbass who doesn't know enough to mind his own damn business."

"Because you're a good man who refused to stand by and watch a father gunned down in front of his children. There's a word for that, you know."

"And it doesn't apply to me. Did you really pick a fight with the cops? Or did I dream that?"

"Sort of? They didn't want to let me through. I had to show them the pictures of us on my phone. Um…" She poked at the remote, dropping the bed rail. "I should warn you, we need more chocolate for Dylan. Like, a store's worth."

"Because—?"

Heat flooded her cheeks. "Well, she received calls from the company, the U.S. Consulate in Munich, and the hospital, because she's your next of kin. And then she called me. I tried to reassure her, but I'm not sure how effective I was."

"Ouch. Definitely more chocolate."

"And a rep from the company called Mr. Wilson."

"What, directly?"

"I think they called his office, but he returned the call himself."

Dan thumped his head against the pillow. "Right after he told me to stop working and enjoy the holiday." He glanced at her sidewise. "Think he'll fire me for disobeying his instructions?"

"Well, he arranged for this nifty private room and the company's covering your medical bills, so I think you're safe. From him, anyway."

"Are we about to fight? When I'm lying here all injured and pathetic?"

He aimed artfully contrived puppy dog eyes her way, and a smile bubbled to her lips.

"You couldn't be pathetic if you tried. And...I'm not sure? I mean, I'm furious at you for just...hurling yourself in front of a gun, but at the same time, I just want to hold you and never let go."

"I could get on board with that." He rolled his shoulder and grimaced.

"Are you all right? Should I ring for the nurse?"

"I'm sore, but I don't think they'll give me anything since I whacked my head."

She scanned the whiteboard beside his bed. Thankfully the notes were in English as well as German. "It says acetaminophen as needed. I think you can ask the nurse the next time they check on you."

He looked at her from under his lashes. "Or you could kiss it better."

She wrinkled her nose at the whiff of stale sweat and antiseptic, tinged with a hint of body odor. "Maybe after you've had a shower."

"You could help me with that."

"So could the orderly who's built like a linebacker."

"Not my type."

She folded her arms on the edge of the bed and rested her chin on them, smell notwithstanding. "I need to bring my laptop so you can call Dylan."

"Why? Is my phone broken? It was in the inside pocket of my jacket."

"I don't know. They handed me a bag with whatever was in your pockets, but I just shoved it inside my tote. I was a bit distracted, you understand."

"So I'll use your phone."

"She specifically said she wants a video call. I think she needs to see for herself that you're all right." She smothered a yawn in her elbow. "I know I did."

"So you're both mad at me?"

"Pretty much."

"Lacey…I'm not sure what you want me to say."

"Neither am I, really. But…you could have come with me to find the police. You didn't have to put yourself at risk."

He toyed with a lock of her hair. "Honestly…I'm not sure I could have walked away. Not now. Before I met you, before Henry Wilson gave me this chance— sure. I'd have faded into the crowd and never looked back. No problem. Hell, I'd never have been in a place full of kids and families at all."

"You could have died—"

"I got winged, that's all."

"They had guns." She sat up straight, dislodging his

hand. "You got shot. It could have been so much worse. You could have left me alone because you risked yourself for people you don't even know." She shuddered and wrapped her arms around herself.

The breath whooshed out of him and he stared at his lap for a long, long moment. Finally, he raised his eyes and stared past her at the blank wall. "Your dad spent his entire career risking himself for strangers."

"And I almost lost him. Look—he was a cop. It was his job, and I had no say in the matter. But you and me—if we're gonna talk about marriage and kids and a life together, we need to talk about this, too. I need to know you won't run off and get yourself killed and leave me all alone."

He turned back from the fascinating wall and studied her. "Lacey, I can't promise that. No one can." He extended his hand, palm up, across the mattress. He looked at her, then at his empty hand. "I spent most of my life being a selfish bastard."

A tiny smile crept across her face and she set her hand in his. "I think Dylan would disagree with your assessment."

"Old me didn't think beyond me and her. Old me wouldn't have dreamed of getting between a guy I don't know and a bullet." He tilted his hand, lacing their fingers together. "But then I met you. Part of falling in love with you was making promises—to me, to you, and yeah, even to the Wilsons."

That's news.

"What did you promise them?"

"To stay on the right side of the law. And—corny as it sounds—to be worthy of you. For all the stuff I did to keep me and Dylan alive, I never once lied to her about the important things. And I can't lie to you either. I can't say I love you and want to have a family with you, then watch some other family get blown away." He squeezed her fingers in a painfully tight grip. "Can you understand that?"

She focused on their clasped hands. Her fingers were turning red, but she didn't try to free her hand. "I want to be selfish. I want you to promise me you'll never ever do anything like that again, but I can't." She raised her gaze to meet his. "It's not fair to expect you to be a good man, then complain when you are. Just…if you can…if there's ever another…oh, hell…can you just stop for a second—just a second—and see if there's another way?"

He chuckled and tugged their hands closer. She stood and hitched herself up on the edge of the bed.

"I will. I promise. Believe me, I do not want to make a habit of getting shot. It hurts too damn much."

Her lips curled in a smirk and she leaned in. "I believe you mentioned something about kissing it better?"

The door banged open and the lights brightened and she damn near fell off the bed.

A rather rotund nurse wearing cotton candy pink scrubs stood in the doorway, clipboard in hand. "*Guten morgen*, Herr Lewis. I'm your day nurse, Gretel. How are you feeling today?"

****

Early morning sunlight glinted off the gilt trim on the *Schöner Brunnen* fountain. The kitschy souvenir shop hadn't rolled out their racks of postcards yet and the wind whipped discarded coffee cups and other bits of debris along the gutters.

Breakfast was cooking in a café nearby, filling the air with tantalizing aromas of coffee and bacon. Lacey's stomach growled.

How long has it been since that beer and pretzel? I should eat something. And sleep before I go back to the hospital.

Still, the crisp air was refreshing after the miasma of hospital odors, and the idea of returning to the stuffy hotel room alone was less than appealing.

Just a few more minutes.

Even if it was weird being alone in a strange city for the first time in months. The deserted streets made it easy to picture lords and ladies in furs and long velvet cloaks sweeping across the cobblestones. Lacey fiddled with the zoom setting on her camera, trying to capture the essence of the square without any twenty-first-century influence.

"*Guten tag.*"

Lacey bit back a curse and nearly fumbled the camera, even though the voice was feminine and soft. "Sorry."

"I am sorry, Fräulein. I did not mean to startle you." The newcomer was a young woman with elaborately curled blonde hair and impeccable makeup.

Heat rushed to her cheeks.

I've been awake all night and I'm still wearing last night's beer. Charming.

"Are you all right?" She was a bit taller than Lacey, with an open, friendly smile.

"I've been up all night at the hospital with a friend." *Why did I say that? I don't even know this girl.* "I was…trying to clear my head."

The girl's clear blue eyes lit with curiosity. "Are you American?"

Lacey nodded.

"I am going there to study for a semester—at a university in Chicago."

"Your English is excellent."

"*Danke*—thank you. I've never gone so far from home before. It's very exciting, isn't it?"

"I think so."

"Were you scared? The first time you traveled alone, I mean."

"More…out of my element than scared, I guess." She tucked her camera away in her bag. "But then I met some great friends. I tried a lot of things I'd never done before. I ate weird food—well, some of it, anyway. I went to an opera." *I met Dan.* "It was…it *is* the best thing that's ever happened to me."

"It sounds wonderful."

A genuine smile crept across her face. "It is."

The girl gazed at the colorful figures on the fountain. "This is my favorite time to come here. I love the market, of course, but when it is quiet like this, it is almost as if— "

"As if people from a storybook are going to walk around the corner?"

"Exactly. Have you come to make a wish?"

"I—we—already did that." She chuckled ruefully. "I'm a little short to reach the ring by myself."

"I can reach it. I may not have my wings on yet, but I can help you make a wish."

Wings?

"You're the *Christkindl*."

"I am, but you may call me Caroline." Her musical accent rendered it as "Karoleena."

"I'm Lacey. So you're like the city's goodwill

ambassador?"

No wonder she's going overseas to school.

Caroline nodded. "I appear here at the market and at events in the community. This is my second year. Next Christmas it will be someone else's turn."

"Will you miss it?" Lacey asked impulsively. She liked this girl—she was sort of like Jenny but without the superior attitude.

"*Ja.* It is a wonderful thing, the way children's faces light up when they see my wings and crown."

"And all the little girls want to be you when they grow up?"

"I know I did. Come, let us make your wish." Caroline reached up and touched the golden ring—not as easily as Dan, but she didn't have to climb the fence, either. She extended her hand to Lacey. "I am going to wish for your friend to be well."

"So am I."

Caroline turned the ring the requisite three times, then released Lacey's hand and stepped away. "Do you have any advice for me for when I go to America?"

Lacey grinned. "Eat the weird food—well, unless it's vegetables." She wrinkled her nose. "Walk in the rain, try new things, and take a million pictures."

"Anything else?"

"Just…believe in yourself…and follow your heart."

****

The hotel room was exactly as they'd left it the day before—and still entirely too hot. Lacey didn't have the energy to deal with it. The message light on the room phone was flashing, and she didn't have the energy to deal with that either.

She dropped the plastic hospital bag with the

remains of Dan's clothes on the couch and it slid right to the floor.

Just as well I can't actually sit on this stupid sofa. If it were remotely comfortable, I'd collapse and fall asleep for a day or so.

She needed to send out her coat for dry cleaning, organize a batch of regular laundry, find a clean outfit for Dan to wear when she picked him up tomorrow, and get him a heavy sweater or something until they could replace his jacket.

Tears prickled her eyes and she pressed the heels of her hands against them.

No hysterics. You've got stuff to do. Right. Deep breath.

Laundry bags and tickets were usually in the closet. She slipped off her coat and rifled through the pockets, then tossed it on a chair, where it miraculously stayed. She added her sweater to the pile since she'd used the cuffs to scrub her face more times than she cared to admit.

Dan, with his usual attention to detail, had started a laundry bag and ticket with each item entered in his meticulous block handwriting. On impulse, she grabbed the last shirt he'd slept in and scratched it off the list. By the time she'd called the front desk for pickup and handed off the laundry to an overly cheerful employee, she was swaying on her feet. She barely remembered to check the lock before she shut off the lights and pulled the drapes shut.

She changed into Dan's shirt and grabbed both their phones to plug into the bedside charger. His phone flared to life when she plugged it in. The lock screen was the picture Mrs. Wilson had taken of the two of them in front of Trevi Fountain. It was the first picture he'd stood still for—mostly because Martha Wilson was an implacable force of nature when it came to matters of the heart. She'd sensed the possibilities between them almost before they did.

Lacey stared at the picture until the screen faded to black. Then she climbed into bed and curled around Dan's pillow.

Chapter Fifteen

"Home sweet…suite."

Lacey hung the Do Not Disturb tag and locked the door. Her freshly dry-cleaned plastic-wrapped coat hung on the rack beside the door, and two extravagant gift baskets and a bunch of balloons occupied the coffee table.

"What's all this?"

"One's from the company and the other is from the family. Why don't you sit and read the cards?"

"On that thing?" He eyed the funky sofa and shuddered. "I'll never get up again."

"We need to replace your jacket. You can't go running around Germany and Austria in December without one."

"I liked that jacket."

She rolled her eyes. "I know. You liked it enough to wear it in Madrid when everyone else was melting."

You were wearing it the first time I saw you.

"ER medics are much too good at hacking clothing to pieces."

"Well, if you could maybe refrain from jumping in front of loaded guns it wouldn't be an issue."

A muscle in his jaw twitched.

Calm down. You already said all of this. Just be grateful he's okay.

She squeezed her eyes shut for a moment. "Sorry."

"Don't be. We talked about this. I scared you. You have every right to be upset."

"I don't have the right to be a harpy about it. You apologized. And you didn't set out to hurt me—you were protecting a family."

He held out his good arm. "Truce?"

She slid her arms around his waist and laid her head on his chest. "Truce." His heartbeat thrummed warm and steady beneath her cheek.

He's here...he's safe.

"So, any preferences for buying a jacket, or should I ask the concierge for recommendations?"

"Can my preference be to deal with it tomorrow? I can't face stores full of rampaging holiday shoppers today."

"Yup—especially since your discharge instructions say for you to take it easy for a few days. How're you feeling?"

"Grubby. I want a shower."

She fluttered her eyelashes vapidly. "Nurse Gretel and Franz the linebacker were both very enthusiastic about the prospect of giving you a sponge bath."

"Yeah, but neither of them is you." He kissed the top of her head and fumbled the buttons of the navy and gray cardigan she'd purchased for him. "This looks like something out of Mr. Wilson's closet." He slid his arm out of the sling and dropped it on the couch, where it promptly slithered to the floor.

She slipped a few of the buttons loose and helped him remove the sweater. "It looks like something much less painful to get on and off than raising a bandaged arm over your head."

"Did they fix the thermostat? I've been in here a

whole minute and I don't have heat stroke yet."

"Maybe? I think they were supposed to send someone—again—after I left this morning. It does feel much more comfortable." She took off her velvet evening wrap and draped it over the back of a chair.

The tiny shirt buttons were even more problematic to undo one-handed. Lacey took pity on him and tugged his shirt tails free, then finished opening the buttons. "Go take your shower. I've got a call to make."

"Dylan?"

She shook her head. "Mrs. Wilson. We'll call Dylan together once you're presentable."

"You're not gonna help wash my back?"

"Play your cards right and I'll join you when I finish my call. Do you need help wrapping your arm?"

He shrugged out of his blue linen shirt and examined the bandage. "Probably? The angle's kinda awkward."

As always, the sight of a shirtless Dan was well worth a long perusal. Just enough muscle definition to be interesting made her palms itch to touch him. And maybe help him out of his jeans so she could see the rest of the package.

No. Nope. Behave yourself. At least until you finish your calls.

He caught her about-to-drool expression and smirked. She shook her head and pointed to the bathroom. "Go get started. I'll be in to wrap your arm."

****

Martha Wilson's smiling face filled Lacey's screen. As always, her hair was perfectly arranged in neat silver waves. She wore a mint-green sweater that looked soft as a cloud and a double strand of pearls. "Lacey, dear, it's so good to see you! And how is Dan?"

"He's fine. He was released from the hospital this morning."

"Good. Henry told me what happened. You must have been so terribly frightened."

"I was, but everything turned out okay. That's what matters."

"I want to hear all about your sister's wedding. I read the society pages, of course. You looked lovely, although that dress was a bit old for you. Whatever was your sister thinking?" She paused, studying Lacey's image. "You look tired, dear. And why are you sitting on the floor?"

"The thermostat in our room was broken, so I haven't been sleeping well—even before Dan's accident. And the furniture in this place is really weird."

"Oh, my. We'll have to look into that. I don't like the idea of our guests staying in uncomfortable accommodations. How are you enjoying the holiday tour? It's one of my favorites."

"Well, it's been int—"

An earsplitting yowl echoed through the suite.

"Good heavens! What—"

Lacey shoved the laptop aside and scrambled to her feet. "Dan? What happened? Did you fall?" She wrenched open the bathroom door.

Dan stood dripping on the mat, clutching a towel around his waist and swearing under his breath. "There's no hot water."

Lacey grabbed another velvety-soft olive-green towel and draped it around his shoulders. "What happened? Did you turn the handle the wrong way?" *Crap. Maybe I shouldn't have left him alone in here.* She stuck her hand into the shower, then snatched it back, flinching from the icy spray. She turned the handle in both directions—no change. She shut off the shower and tried the sink—also frigid. "About that bingo card…"

"About threatening to tell the owners about our lousy rooms…"

"Owners—crap! I've got Mrs. Wilson on a video call. Are you—"

He flapped a hand toward the door. "Go reassure my boss's wife I'm not dead. I'll just skulk in here and see if I can locate the remains of my dignity."

She stepped out and pulled the door shut. Her laptop was squawking from where she'd dropped it on the carpet.

"Lacey? Lacey, what's happening?"

She grabbed the laptop and held it straight. "Hi. Sorry."

"What happened? Is Dan all right?"

"Well, they finally shut off the heat…and apparently the hot water."

On-screen, Martha Wilson pursed her lips. "Start packing your things—no, never mind—we'll ask for a butler or extra bellhops to help you. Henry's on the phone with the general manager. Either they relocate you to a comfortable room or we relocate the entire tour."

There was no arguing with that tone, and honestly she didn't want to. "Okay. Let me get Dan a change of clothes before—"

A brisk knock sounded through the suite.

"Go take care of your young man, and let us know once you're settled in your new room."

"I will. Thanks. For everything. Really."

"Of course, my dear."

****

Dylan started shouting the second the call connected. "Two of you! Two fancy sports watches that do everything but wash the dishes and neither of you can tell time. I've been waiting an hour for this call to go through. I swear I should have let your boss fly me out there just so I could knock both your heads together."

Dan noted guiltily that Dylan had dark rings under her eyes to match Lacey's. Still, where Lacey could be comforted with cuddles, Dylan had perfected a tough shell years ago. He opted for nonchalance, knowing the brief jolt of irritation was better for her than wallowing in fear over what-ifs.

He sat quietly until she ran out of breath. The bed had a padded headboard and the two pillows tucked behind his back made it quite comfortable. "Hello to you too, sister dearest." He recrossed his legs on the bed.

Dylan's eyes narrowed. "Nice robe, Danny boy."

"Thanks. Santa brought it."

"I'll bet she did."

Lacey glanced from the screen to him and mouthed, "behave."

"I'm sorry we're late. We changed rooms."

"They couldn't fix the thermostat? Or was it the door locks?"

"Thermostat. Door locks was the first room we transferred out of." Lacey scooted over so she could see the screen clearly. "And yes. They finally got the heat to go off. As well as the hot water."

"Nice. Why can't you call from the living room like civilized people?"

"So charming. As it happens, I'm on bedrest for the day."

Lacey elbowed him. "This is the hotel with the

weird modern furniture, so if we were in the sitting area, we'd be on the floor and I'd have to haul him up afterward."

"Okay, I take it back. I don't wanna go there unless there's a nice normal American chain motel I can check into."

"Are you sure you don't want to come to Vienna for Christmas? I'll pay for the ticket and a room."

"Thanks, Lacey, but like I told your boss, I'm covering the crisis call center so people can spend the day with their families."

She poked Dan again. "See? It runs in the family."

"Yeah, except I know better than to run in front of a gun. What were you thinking, Danny?"

"I was thinking I couldn't watch a man gunned down, right in front of his kids, a few days before Christmas. You and me, we never had those things. I couldn't watch them get snatched away from those kids. Not when I was standing right there."

Lacey laid a hand on his arm, caressing him through his silk sleeve until his muscles unclenched. "We've had this discussion a few times already."

"Good."

"Look, I'm really sorry about the scary phone calls. I was with him in the treatment room and I was kind of a mess. I didn't realize—"

"It's okay. You must have been terrified."

"They kept trying to boot me out until you told them otherwise."

Dylan eyed them both speculatively. "You know, there's a solution to that particular problem."

Lacey and Dan exchanged slightly guilty glances. "It's…under discussion."

"Finally." Dylan's gaze shifted to Dan. "You're really all right?"

"I'll be fine. A bandage and a bump on the head. I've had lots worse."

"We both have."

"This doesn't really hurt too much."

Dylan raised an eyebrow.

"I mean, yeah, it hurts. I got shot, of course it hurts, but it doesn't seem as bad as…oh, hell, I sound like a sappy holiday film…"

"Believe it or not, I understand what you mean and it doesn't sound sappy at all."

Lacey looked from one to the other. She held up her hand, finger and thumb about an inch apart. "Maybe just a little bit sappy."

****

Dan dozed while Lacey put away the laptop and plugged in their phones. The mattress dipped as she perched on the edge.

"Hey…wake up for a second and take your meds."

He opened his eyes lazily and accepted the pills and bottle of water. "A whole day of bedrest?"

"At least. The doctor said after that you can use your judgment, but not to push it. Your body needs sleep to repair itself." She tugged the covers up to his chest, then smoothed them.

"And what will you be doing while I'm sleeping the day away?"

"I'm going to be sleeping right next to you."

He wanted to protest wasting a day, but the siren song of the king bed—the only usable piece of furniture in the whole damn hotel—was pulling him under. He relaxed into the embrace of the stack of goose down pillows. *Damn things are pretty comfortable when the room isn't broiling.* After a minute, he sensed the lights dimming, then Lacey slipped into bed beside him. *She's dead on her feet.*

She curled into his uninjured side and lay her head on his shoulder. He wrapped his good arm around her.

"I'm sorry for…all of this," he mumbled.

"It's all right. You're safe. That's all that really matters. There are much worse ways to spend a day or so than curled up in a lovely king bed with room service just a phone call away."

"Maybe, but there're better things we could be doing in this bed than sleeping."

She laughed against his chest. "All in good time. Let's get you well. You know…like you kept telling me for the first half of this trip." Her breathing evened out after a few minutes, and the tension drained out of her body.

He tried to let go and drift off, but it wasn't entirely comfortable, sleeping propped up with his arm resting at his side on its own pillow. Besides which, the two most important ladies in his life were justifiably upset with him.

Dylan would be okay without me. She always was the smart one. She's got a solid job and her own network of friends now. And she's right. As usual.

There was a very simple way to prevent the hospital staff barring Lacey from his treatment decisions or what must have been terrifying phone calls to Dylan.

But am I ready for that? Are we?

"Mmmmff?" Lacey's fingers curled around a fold of his shirt.

"Shhh…" He pressed his lips to the crown of her

head. "Go back to sleep, babe."

She has every right to be upset. She uprooted her whole life to travel with me, and I could have left her on her own—and right after we faced the possibility of little Plus Two.

Gradually, her warmth seeped into him, and his tension eased. He hadn't slept well in the hospital, between the lack of Lacey and the lack of privacy. Now though, he had everything he needed.

But do I deserve it?

Chapter Sixteen

Crowds at Vienna International had thinned out for the night. The last few planes had emptied and the passengers dispersed to their respective destinations. Empty baggage carousels continued their endless revolutions. Overnight janitorial crews called cheerful greetings to one another as they hauled their vacuums and mop buckets onto the concourse. Dolce Vita's luxurious teal motor coach departed for their hotel—minus two guests.

Most of the service desks along the curved glass-enclosed corridor had shut down for the night—except for the tastefully appointed Dolce Vita office. Two Christmas trees trimmed with teal baubles and sparkling golden fairy lights framed the entrance, and a rack of stunning full-color brochures for upcoming tours dominated one wall. Large framed posters of the ubiquitous Dolce Vita teal motor coach stopped in front of iconic landmarks around the globe graced the other walls.

A passing security patrol called out a greeting to the single rep still on duty. She waved and turned her attention to the couple in front of her.

Lacey perched on a surprisingly comfortable teal armchair. "Are you sure?"

"I'm afraid so, Miss Devere. They've checked the luggage hold of the plane and the baggage claim area.

We will, of course, reach out to our office at the Nuremberg airport."

Out on the concourse, a floor polisher whirred to life.

Dan laid his good hand over hers. "We've got receipts for the bags we checked."

The Dolce Vita rep pushed her glasses up on her nose with an index finger. "Yes, sir. According to the computer, it was checked through and loaded."

"Except it obviously wasn't."

She slid a zippered pouch in the ubiquitous Dolce Vita teal across the polished wooden desk. "I can give you a travel kit if that would help?"

Lacey shook her head. "It's my garment bag that's missing. All three of my good dresses—and we're going to a ball on New Year's Eve."

The rep winced, then recovered her professional smile. "How about some chocolate?"

"That, we'll take," Dan replied, accepting the shiny gold box tied with teal ribbons.

He winked at Lacey, and her lip curled in a small smirk. They both knew Dolce Vita stocked the good stuff for service recovery.

"I'm sure your bag will be located in plenty of time. Let's fill out the claim forms, just in case." The rep opened a document on her computer.

Lacey thumped her head against Dan's good shoulder. "Someday we'll laugh about this, right?"

"Three messed up hotels, one thwarted robbery, and one lost bag? That'll make a helluva story."

"I've got a car waiting to take you to the hotel as soon as we finish this. You'll be much more comfortable there."

"I hope so," Dan muttered.

****

They were staying at the "fairy castle" hotel again. The doorman bowed and a waft of spicey pine scent from the fresh greenery tickled Dan's nose as they entered.

Christmas trees of various sizes adorned in shades of blue, white, and silver replaced the cream and pink floral displays from their previous stay. A majestic gingerbread castle held pride of place on a satin-draped display table in the center of the lobby—thankfully with no rampaging soccer fans to destroy it.

Tasteful instrumental holiday music played quietly over the sound system. Everything was neat and polished and in its place. An aura of peaceful late-night quiet prevailed.

The desk clerk smiled broadly and gestured to an enticing tower of pale blue and white macarons which stood on the front desk. "*Gruss Gott.*"

"*Gruss Gott,*" Lacey replied, reaching for a cookie.

Dan adjusted his sling irritably. "Dan Lewis and Lacey Devere, with the Dolce Vita holiday tour."

"Of course, sir. We understand from your hostess that one of your bags has yet to arrive. We took the liberty of prechecking you into your suite and having the remainder of your luggage delivered. Your bathroom is fully stocked with complimentary toiletries, but if there is anything else we can supply, please call and we will be more than happy to assist you." He tapped a few keys on his computer, then slid a key pack across the counter.

Dan eyed it suspiciously. "You have our reservation?"

"Certainly, Herr Lewis. Dolce Vita travelers are among our most elite guests. We are delighted to welcome you and will of course do whatever we can to assist you with your stay."

Dan still didn't take the key pack. "And this is for a clean room?"

The bewildered clerk nodded.

"With no one else in it?"

Another nod.

"The door locks? And the world champion sports ball fans aren't having a wild party on our floor?"

The clerk edged subtly away from the desk.

"The building's not on fire?"

"Perhaps Herr Lewis would care to speak to the manager on duty?"

A security guard dressed in a dark blue blazer emerged from the back office. He nodded pleasantly while exuding a distinct aura of "don't mess with me."

Lacey laid her warm hand on Dan's good arm and squeezed gently while offering a bright smile to the desk clerk. "I'm sure it's fine. We've had…issues…with our accommodations this trip."

The clerk stared at her wide-eyed. "Apparently so."

"And on that note, the missing piece of luggage is my garment bag. It's got my gown for the New Year's Eve ball, so I'd appreciate a call whenever it's delivered. The night manager can wake me up—I don't care. I just want to know it's safe."

"Of course, Fräulein. Should you wish, our concierge would be happy to provide a list of fine clothing establishments in the area."

"I hope that won't be necessary but thank you. Are there any parcels for us?"

The clerk checked his computer. "Not at this time. Should any arrive, they will be delivered to your suite."

"Thank you. You've been very helpful." She elbowed Dan.

"Yeah…thanks."

****

Dan slumped onto a couch covered in elaborate ice-blue brocade. His movements dislodged several slippery satin cushions, which tumbled to the floor. A Christmas tree decorated with shimmering blue glass baubles and white velvet ribbon swags stood in the corner. Glittering silver icicles tipped the branches. Fairy lights draping the tree and mantel cast a soft glow over the space.

Lacey returned from a walk-through of their suite and sat next to him, sending even more cushions cascading to the carpet. "Hey, guess what? It's a nice clean room, with no one else in it, it's a reasonable temperature, the doors lock, and there's hot water. How's that for a Christmas miracle?"

"It looks like a blue satin cushion factory exploded in here," he grumbled.

"If they'd exploded, the room would be full of feathers, which it isn't and please don't give the universe any ideas. It has enough of its own." She nestled into his side, filling his senses with hints of lavender and warmth. "It's a beautiful room, we can sit on the furniture, and the tub is big enough for both of us."

"And I can't soak in it."

You're being a jerk. You realize that, right?

She rolled her eyes. "You can rest your arm on a towel on the edge. There's lots of plush blue and white towels. The velvety kind."

He snorted. "I'm still waiting for the other shoe to drop."

She toyed with the buttons on his shirt. "You know,

right this second, you're reminding me of a very particular holiday character, and it's not a flattering one."

He exhaled explosively and sagged against the back of the sofa. "I'm sorry. It's just…this whole trip, everything's gone sideways."

"And now we're here in a lovely room and it's almost Christmas and can we please just try to enjoy ourselves? Please?"

Chapter Seventeen

"And step-two-three, turn-two-three—"

A Strauss waltz played softly from Lacey's laptop as she turned around the room, arms raised in an approximation of a waltz hold. *How the heck does this work when one partner only has full use of one arm? What if he still needs the sling?* She'd turned off the chandeliers, bathing the room in a pleasant twilight from a few table lamps set on low. Her shadow chased itself around the top edge of the walls.

The bathroom door opened behind her. "Strauss? Really?"

She smiled over her shoulder. "It's not like you can escape it around here. It sorta grew on me. People are allowed to like different things, right?"

"They are, indeed. You know, like so many other things, that works better when both of us are doing it together."

She completed a turn and saw him lounging in the doorframe, arms crossed, subtly supporting the injured one. The blue silk pajama pants sat a bit low on his hips and her gaze lingered. "If I'd known this was going to be such a loungewear-intensive trip, I'd have gotten you more than one set."

He sauntered across the room and took her hand, bowing over it before bestowing a kiss. "There's another sort of dancing we could be practicing right now."

"Oh, really?"

"Mm-hmm. One that won't strain my arm...and doesn't require loungewear."

She stepped closer and tipped her chin up. "Or any other kind of wear?"

"Well, one small...accessory...as it were."

"From that shop in Amsterdam?"

His gaze swept over her from head to toe and she felt her cheeks turn pink. The straps on the lavender silk nightie never stayed put on her shoulders, a fact Dan seemed to appreciate. She trailed a hand over his chest, tracing nicely understated muscles. He was warm and solid and alive beneath her hand.

He wrapped his good arm around her waist and turned them toward the bed. "See? This works." He kissed her temple. "It'll be fine." He started to raise his injured arm and winced.

"Dan..."

"It's fine." Another kiss. "We've got a whole week before the ball, and we're going to the dance class with the rest of the group." He bumped into the bed and sat down, pulling her between his legs. "Now"—his hot breath fanned across her throat, followed by surprisingly soft lips—"is this really what you want to be worrying about right now?"

She tilted her head, giving him a better angle. "No...no it isn't. But are you sure—"

He laid gentle fingers over her mouth. "We've spent the bulk of this trip waiting for news and waiting for packages and room repairs—"

"And luggage."

"And luggage. And waiting for one or the other of us to be in...prime operating condition." His hand slipped to her hip and flexed a bit, so warm through the thin silk. "I think we both know we're never going to have the kind of picture-perfect life that gets made into TV movies." He tugged her closer. "But what we have is pretty damn amazing. And I think we should embrace it."

"Embrace it, huh?" She draped her arms over his shoulders, mindful of the bandage.

Dan trailed his lips along her throat to her shoulder, nudging one of the lace straps out of his way. He shifted back onto the bed, fumbling for a place to rest his arm and landing them in a tangled heap.

Her gasp mingled with his pained groan.

"Here—let me—"

"It's fine, babe. I'm not that breakable." Another groan. "I think."

"Let me help, you stubborn idiot." She steered him onto the pillows she'd already stacked against the headboard for him.

"Pot, kettle."

"I mean it. Lean on me—I'm strong enough for both of us."

"I know you are."

She settled him in a comfortable slouch against a mound of pillows, with his arm resting on its own super-firm down-filled monstrosity. "You're not bleeding are you? Do you need anything for the pain?"

He glanced at the bandage. "It's fine. My arm just gets cranky if I lean on it or you know—look at it funny. And I can think of something that would do wonders for the pain."

"What about your head?"

"Still firmly attached."

She glared at him. "You know what I mean. Any

headaches? Blurred vision?"

"No headache and I can see you just fine." His lips curved in a wicked smirk. "So...where were we?"

She blew a loose curl out of her eyes, then ran her hands down his legs, loving the feel of silk over firm muscle, and squeezed his feet. "Suppose you lie back and—"

"Think of England? I could do that. We made pretty good memories there."

She shot him a look—which was probably more sultry than menacing. "And let me do all the work?"

"*All* the work?"

"Okay...most of the work."

"Awfully sure of yourself."

"Oh, I am." She slid off the bed and gathered the hem of her nightgown in her hands, raising it up, inch by inch, until she pulled it off and tossed it in the general direction of a dainty side chair upholstered in icy-blue brocade. Where it promptly slithered to the carpet.

"Are you really gonna make the invalid pick up your stuff from the floor?"

She paused with her thumbs hooked in the band of her lavender silk panties. "Is that really the most interesting thing in this room right now?" She slipped off the panties, letting him get a good long look.

"Not even remotely."

"Good answer." She sashayed over to the left side of the bed and climbed up, crawling over to him with cat-like grace.

His gaze tracked every motion as she knelt beside him. He leaned up on his left elbow and reached across with his right hand, settling on her thigh. He kneaded the muscle, then stroked up over her hip to her ribs, finally dragging the pads of his fingers along the side of her breast.

Her breath caught and a shiver rippled through her. *Damn, he's good at that.* She leaned over him, bracing herself to keep her weight off his injury—but still managing to press her breasts to his chest—and kissed him once before pulling back. She cupped his face in her hand, dragging her thumb across his lower lip. "Hey—before we get too carried away, promise me you'll say something if anything hurts."

He rearranged himself, skimming his hand up and down her spine. "Endorphins are wonderful things."

"Dan." She sat back on her heels, dislodging his hand. "Promise me, or I swear I'll get dressed and go sleep on the couch. We're not in modern furniture hell anymore. I can do that here."

Dan turned puppy dog eyes on her. "And leave me with this…predicament?"

She eyed his "predicament." It was impressive, and promised to be very enjoyable, but… "I have full use of both hands. I can take care of my own predicaments quite nicely. Can you say the same?"

"You drive a hard bargain," he grumbled.

She arched an eyebrow.

"Fine. I promise I'll tell you if I'm in pain. Now can we please…?"

She patted his "predicament" and kissed him lightly on the mouth. "All you had to do was agree with me." She fished under the pillows and retrieved a package.

"A whole box? Ambitious."

"Afraid you can't keep up with me?"

"Oh, I can keep…up…with you all right."

"Well, I can't go to the fancy dinner party in jeans

and a sweater. You have a better idea of how to pass the time without clothing?"

He shrugged—as much as he was able in his current position. "With clothing, without…"

"I think without works better, don't you?" She smirked and set her hands on his waistband.

He smirked right back and lifted his hips so she could slide the pants off and toss them in the general direction of the chair. She selected a condom from the package, then shoved the box under a pillow where it could easily be retrieved.

She eyed her lover, reclining against the pillows like an exquisite marble statue come to life—long legs, the right balance of muscle and strength without being overdone—even the bandage on his arm didn't detract from the image. It was a badge of honor, after all. But it was his eyes that took her breath away, their stormy blue softened in a way only those closest to him ever saw.

And of course, there was another salient feature most of those marble gods had…lost. Her mouth ticked up in a smile-smirk as she rolled the condom on him, then tossed the wrapper on the bedside table.

He made a small sound in the back of his throat when she touched him, then a full-fledged groan when she swung her leg over his hips and sank down on him.

She drew in a shuddering breath and took a moment to adjust to the feel of him. To her horror, tears prickled at her eyes. "I could have lost you."

"You didn't. I'm right here."

And he was—warm and solid and wonderfully alive. *I need this…I need to feel him…to know he's with me. God I sound crazy…* She blinked furiously, then smiled tremulously for him.

He blinked his own suspiciously shiny eyes, then grinned at her. "I'm not going anywhere." He waggled his eyebrows at her. "I couldn't if I wanted to and believe me…I don't want to."

She snorted and her smile morphed into a grin. "Just lie back and let me do all the work." She set one hand on his chest for balance and laced the fingers of her other hand with his.

"Oh, it's work, is it?" He shifted his injured arm, finally settling on tracing idle patterns on her knee with his fingertips.

"You know what I mean." Lacey leaned down and kissed him, her blonde hair tumbling around their faces. She shifted her hips and moved over him in a gentle, sensuous rhythm.

"I'm not all that fragile."

"Patience. We've got all night. Wouldn't want to wear you out." She dipped her head and planted a kiss over his heart.

"Hey—I want you to enjoy this too. Here—wait…" He raised his knees and braced his feet. "How's that?"

"That" was an angle which created blissful friction in all the right places and coaxed an incoherent sound from her throat. *That is…oh, my God…how is he even thinking about me right now?* She blinked, and his clear blue eyes were fixed on hers. *How did I get so lucky?*

"Partners, remember? Besides, I really like this view."

And then he did something with his hips and Lacey lost all track of time and place…at least until every church bell in the city rang out joyously all at once.

****

Dan smirked and brushed a lock of hair behind her

ear as the bells continued to toll. "Wow. I mean, I know I'm impressive but—"

"Pretty sure they're ringing in Christmas Day, you ass." She lifted herself off him and curled into his side, panting as though she'd run a marathon.

That was incredible. Even for us. The condom could wait a few minutes until his legs were ready to hold him. He pressed his lips to her temple. "I like my story better."

"That was…" She gasped, still trying to catch her breath. "I never tried that before."

"Me neither."

She stared at him.

"I never…" *Crap. How do I say this?* "There's never been anyone I—" *I'm saying this all wrong.*

She caught his hand and laced their fingers together. "Hey—we're grownups here. I never imagined I was your first."

"You are." *Smooth, Dan.* "I mean…you're the first person I ever let get close enough…the first one important enough for me to want to make sure…" He sucked in a deep breath and tried again. "I want to make you happy."

She raised their intertwined hands to her lips. "You do."

"I want to make you feel good."

"Oh, you definitely did that."

"I know we're not ready for little Plus Two yet, but there's no reason we can't…practice. With suitable precautions in place, of course."

Lacey slid a hand under her pillow. "Got a whole box of precautions right here. And you know what they say—practice makes perfect."

He sat up, and Lacey was right there, steadying him.

"I'm gonna go get cleaned up."

"Hurry back. I've got an experiment in mind."

He turned at the bathroom door. "Oh?"

"Maybe you *were* the reason all those bells were ringing. Only one way to find out."

Chapter Eighteen

Mr. Wilson smiled genially at the screen. "Good to see you, Dan. I hope you and Lacey had a wonderful Christmas."

Dan carefully schooled his features, grateful for the closed door between him and the extremely rumpled bed. *My employer does not need to know how we spent the day.* "It was very enjoyable, sir."

"Good…good. How are you feeling?" He took a sip from a mug shaped like a snowman, then set it on a matching napkin. His study looked as cozy as the last time, minus the enormous stacks of gifts that had been under the tree.

"Much better. The medic has me down to a smaller dressing. He says I can do whatever's comfortable, except swim or soak in a tub." *Or get too creative when we…nope. He doesn't need to know that.*

"I'm glad to hear it. Officially, I'm supposed to remind you you're not a police officer and you probably should have stayed out of it."

"Of course, sir. I understand."

Mr. Wilson waved a hand dismissively. "Personally…Dan, I'm very proud of you. And if the benefits office gives you any trouble about your expenses, you come to me and I'll cover them myself."

"Thank you, sir. That…means a lot."

I went decades without hearing those words.

"Now, I know I said no more business until after the holidays, but I have some information I wanted to share." He leaned back in his chair and steepled his hands together.

A lifetime of practice kept Dan's features impassive, even as adrenaline flooded his system.

Mr. Wilson continued, seemingly oblivious. Although he could never really tell—the old man was very sharp.

"My contact with the Italian authorities passed along news I knew you'd be interested in. There was another robbery—a female tourist with another tour company. She met a man supposedly from her group, they returned to her room, drank heavily, and the following morning she woke up alone, and minus several pieces of jewelry."

Dan blinked, digesting that information. "So—"

"So, this is obviously the work of a local perpetrator. My contact is reaching out to the police in the area to see if there are any more reports of similar incidents." He blew on the contents of his mug and took another sip. "I told you I didn't suspect you, and I meant it, but I thought you'd be pleased to know there's proof now."

Dan released a long, slow breath, trying not to visibly sag.

"Now then…where are you staying? No issues with the hotel this time?"

He relaxed and chuckled. "The hotel is fine. It's the one the ladies think is a fairy tale castle."

"With the blue satin ruffles all over everything?" Mr. Wilson shook his head. "I swear I lose a pair of slippers every time we stay there."

"Maybe, but it has hot water, functioning HVAC, and a charming lack of drunk sports fans."

"And has the airline returned Lacey's bag?"

"Not yet. She's starting to worry. All the stores are closed today, and the ones she talked to are out of stock on formal wear until after the holidays."

"Which does nothing to outfit her for the New Year's Eve ball. I'll see if Martha has any ideas. She's got favorite shops in all the cities we frequent. She might be able to pull some strings."

"I'd appreciate that. Things have been a bit chaotic this trip, and I'd really like something to go according to plan."

"The group is signed up for a dance class, right? You should go. The Viennese waltz is rather energetic, and you might have trouble with your arm. The instructor should be able to help. And if not, the two of you certainly have a gift for improvisation."

I suppose that's one way of putting it.

****

"How was your Christmas, sis?"

Dylan nodded thoughtfully. "It was good. I didn't have any major issues to deal with...mostly people with no families who just wanted someone to talk to. And hey—your boss is amazing."

"Oh?"

She chugged from an oversized mug and gulped the contents. "They made a hefty donation to the center and sent a bunch of catered food for the staff. It was really nice of them."

"Yeah...they're good people."

"So what did you get Lacey for Christmas?"

He kept his expression and tone perfectly bland. "An assortment of really good wool socks."

She nearly spit on her screen. "Are you kidding

me?"

"No."

"Socks. Your first Christmas together and you got her socks?"

"She complained her toes were cold, so I got her some top-quality wool socks. What's wrong with that?"

Dylan's eyes narrowed. "What did you really get her?"

"Nothing I'm going to share with you. You'll jump to conclusions and they'll be wrong. Lacey can tell you herself if she wants to—when her gift arrives, which it hasn't yet."

Because I haven't had a chance to go shopping.

Dylan scrubbed a hand over her face in a painfully familiar gesture. "You subjected her to a trip filled with screwed-up hotels, lost luggage, and you getting shot, and all you got her was socks and a mystery gift that isn't even there yet? Do they sell chocolate in Vienna? 'Cuz I suggest you go buy *a lot*."

****

Mrs. Wilson sipped from a dainty holly-patterned teacup, then set it carefully on a matching saucer. The rest of the festive tea set and a tiered server full of sugar-dusted cookies sat on a rolling cart behind her chair. "And how is Dan doing?"

"He's much better, thanks. Grumpy because he can't swim, but I figure that's a good sign."

"And are you planning on taking a dance class before the ball? The Viennese waltz is rather different from American social dancing. The classes are really quite enjoyable."

"We should, if only so we can figure out how to dance with his arm in a sling. Of course, it may all be for nothing—the airline still hasn't found my dress bag."

"Surely you can get a new dress?"

"Unfortunately, no. Every place I've called has been sold out for the season, and of course today is a local holiday."

"What about Hans's boutique?"

"Nope, not even him."

Mrs. Wilson suddenly looked every bit as formidable as her husband. She set down her teacup with a clink. "We'll see about that."

****

"So I made myself one of them steaks when I got home from your sister's, and I used the bottle opener you sent me—I guarantee I'll never lose that one, the little red wooden shoe is too hard to miss—for some German beer I ordered special. So it was sorta like you were here with me."

"You got the box from Amsterdam?"

"It was delivered late Christmas Eve, so I brought Jenny's package with me."

She pressed her lips together and raised one eyebrow. *Here it comes...*

"Her husband—Mike? Mitch?"

"Marvin."

"Yeah...his great-grandma was Dutch and he really liked those ornaments you sent. He hung 'em right on the front of the tree with some family heirlooms."

Huh. Maybe he's got a backbone after all.

"You look a little down. Everything okay?"

She manufactured a smile. "Everything's wonderful, Daddy. Really. Well, except that the airline lost the bag with all my good dresses and we have tickets for a ball on New Year's Eve."

"A ball? Like in a fairy tale?"

"Yup. That's a thing here."

"Can't you just buy a new dress?"

She laughed a little. "It's not that easy. Every place is sold out for the holidays."

"Hey, I know—I can send your dress from the wedding."

"No!" She lowered her voice and schooled her expression. "I mean, don't bother."

"It's no trouble, honey. I got plenty of pictures. I'll even find the shoes and purse and whatever you're wearing in the pictures and take it to one of those places where they pack and ship stuff."

"No, really. It, uh wouldn't get here in time."

"Hey, it's a special occasion—I don't mind paying extra."

"I'm in Vienna, Dad. There's no way it would get here." *And no way I'm wearing that thing again. Ever.* "Anyway, there's a dress code. I need to wear a full-length gown and that dress is tea length."

"Nuts. I just wish I could help, sweetheart."

"I know. We'll figure it out."

"So what did you and your fella do for Christmas?"

Oh, I am so not answering that!

"We…stayed in. Dan's still got his arm in a sling, and my dinner dress is in the missing bag."

"That's too bad. He sounds like a good guy with a good heart. That's all I ever wanted for you, Lacey. But I gotta say—he's a private security consultant for a swanky travel company—he's still a civilian, not a street cop. He shoulda stayed out of it."

Nope. Not explaining that either.

"I know, Daddy. But it happened so fast, and all he

could think of was that he didn't want a father to get hurt—especially right before Christmas, with his kids right there."

Dad looked dubious, but generally pleased. "Well, as long as you're both all right. You gotta bring him here to meet me sometime. I wanna shake his hand."

"And then give him the shovel speech?" She shook her head with a fond smile. "I'm a little old for that."

"Nah, you're still my baby girl. Anyway, did he get you anything special for Christmas?"

Nope, nope, nope.

She struggled to keep her voice level, even though her cheeks felt ready to combust from heat. "We try to keep gifts small or useful."

"Oh, right. The luggage thing. But he musta got you something?"

"He got me the most amazing wool socks."

"Socks?" He snorted. "Even I got your mother something better than socks our first Christmas together."

"And were you and Mom walking around outside all day in Europe in December? I complained my toes were cold, and he did something about it. What's wrong with that?"

"Not a thing, sweetheart."

****

"Budge up."

Dan patted her feet and she curled her knees so he could sit on the other end of the sofa. Which of course sent a pile of cushions slithering to the floor.

"How were your calls?" He rubbed her calf absently.

"Good. Dad loved his presents, and Mrs. Wilson is going to talk to her favorite local shop about a dress.

You?"

"Dylan had a quiet holiday."

Lacey leaned up on her elbows. "But that's good, right? Quiet at a crisis center?"

"It is."

"So what aren't you telling me? How was your call with Mr. Wilson?"

"He had some news about Italy. Turns out, there's been more robberies since we left. At least one other victim from another tour group. Local authorities are trying to determine if there have been more."

"So you're officially off the hook?"

He nodded.

She let her gaze drift over him from head to toe. "So as soon as you get the bandage off, I get to ogle you in that black swimsuit again?"

"Only if I get to ogle you in that red two-piece."

"I think that can be arranged."

Chapter Nineteen

Lacey squinted against the late-December sun glittering on plate-glass windows in the old city's finest shopping district. Wind whistled among the gracious stone buildings and scuttled the odd bit of trash along the cobbled streets.

Dan shivered on the steps waiting to be admitted to the building where Hans's boutique was located. Lacey noticed and slipped her arms around his waist. "I'm sorry your new jacket didn't arrive yet."

He shrugged with his good shoulder. "The delivery people are in cahoots with the doctors, trying to keep me in bed."

"And is that such a bad thing?"

His smirk and the sparkle in his eye promised a not-so-safe-for-public response, which was interrupted by the apologetic doorman ushering them inside.

Hans greeted them in the foyer of his boutique. Lacey bit the inside of her cheek to keep a straight face as he bustled toward them in a suit the color of café au lait, combined with navy-blue accents and another blindingly white shirt. *At least it's not pink, like the last trip. Seriously, does he wear those shirts just once? Nothing looks that white after being laundered.*

"*Gruss Gott,* Fräulein Lacey." He took her hands and offered air kisses to both cheeks. "You are as lovely as ever."

"*Gruss Gott*, Hans."

He turned to Dan. "And this must be your very own Prince Charming. *Gruss Gott*."

Dan extended his left hand and Hans shook it, albeit awkwardly.

"Frau Wilson told me about your very heroic injury. So fortunate for that family you were there."

Dan flinched slightly at the word "heroic." "I'm just glad I could help."

She squeezed his arm. "And I'm glad he's all right."

Hans took Lacey's hand in both of his. "I must apologize for the confusion when you first called. You must have spoken to the new receptionist, who is not yet familiar with our select clientele."

Damn, I hope no one got in trouble. "It's fine, really. These things happen." *Especially when it's not even my name on the select clientele list.*

"Frau Wilson tells me the airline lost your dress bag."

Lacey nodded. "All three of my good dresses are in it, including the two we bought here."

"Given time, I can replace those, but as you can see, our stock is quite depleted this week. Still, we shall find you something marvelous." He tilted his head to one side, studying her. "You are not making your debut, correct? So you do not need white?"

"Nope. No debut. No white dress required."

"Well, that makes it easier. Still, had you required a white gown, I would have moved heaven and earth to find one for you."

Dan eyed the profusion of displays in the shop. Mannequins were grouped by color, clustered around ceiling-height Christmas trees decorated with glass balls in coordinating shades. "This looks like an awful lot of 'no dresses.' "

"These are samples from new spring collections," Hans supplied, smoothing his navy-blue paisley tie.

"Meaning what, exactly? They're dresses, aren't they?"

Lacey laid a calming hand on Dan's arm. "It means these are the only ones. There's no stock to pick from, so either I find a dress that fits me or I'm out of luck."

Not that there's a chance in hell of me attending a ball at a palace wearing a two-piece yellow anything with a bare midriff.

"I have called in my best seamstress to assist you, Fräulein Lacey." He nodded toward a matronly woman dressed in a smock with deep pockets. She had a tape measure draped around her neck and wore a pincushion strapped to her wrist.

"If anyone can work a Christmas miracle for you, it is I." He sketched a shallow bow.

"Christmas was two days ago," Dan muttered.

"Will you stop?" Lacey hissed. She examined the displays, walking around the mannequins to get all the details. *Giant flower print—nope. Huge floofy skirts—oh hell no. Oh that looks like it's from the old TV show about the family who lived in the haunted house—but in fire engine red.* She shuddered.

Dan pointed at a two-piece ensemble consisting of a cherry-red off-the-shoulder crop top and a skirt and train printed with huge red roses. "Does that come with a basket of bananas to balance on your head?"

She elbowed him. Gently. "Shush."

Hans looked momentarily affronted, then schooled his features.

Dan leaned in and whispered in her ear. "I think that one is missing a piece. Isn't something supposed to go over the bra?"

She leveled a mock glare at him. "Do I have to make you wait upstairs in the café?"

Mermaid skirts and fishtail trains—nope, not for dancing. That one looks like lingerie. Fluffy pink junior prom dresses—no. Oh, look—there's the silver pearl color the rest of Jenny's bridesmaids wore. Uh-uh.

She paused in front of a plum lamé gown with a simple halter top and full skirt. It…wasn't terrible. It was also plus size and would require extensive alterations. It was a shame to waste all the extra fabric. *And do I really want to settle for "not terrible?"* "Maybe we should just skip the ball. We can always try again next year. Your arm—"

"Will be fine for a few dances. I can rest it in the sling when we're not dancing." He cupped her face in his good hand. "I've been wanting to escort you to one of these things since our first trip. It'll be fine."

"I don't want to spoil it for you—not after everything that went wrong on this trip—but I don't really want to go to another fancy event in a dress I hate."

"Okay, I don't entirely understand that, because I'm not a girl, but if you really can't find something you like, we'll call it quits and stay in on New Year's Eve. But Mrs. Wilson got them to open this place special for you, so make sure you give them a fair shot." He nodded toward a display. "What about those?"

The dresses were blue. Of course they were. *Again with the bare midriff. Again with the no. Ice-blue brocade, strapless—it's gorgeous—and the perfect size for a teenager on a fad diet. Nope. Royal blue velvet...much too large.*

Oh.

She almost missed it—it was toward the back of the display, partially hidden by a tree decked in sparkling blue glass baubles. Midnight blue, off-the-shoulder, with understated beading in a floral motif. *It looks about my size; maybe a little long...*

As if reading her mind, Hans materialized beside her. "The beading thins well above the hem. This could be shortened easily."

The seamstress nodded, fingering her tape measure.

"Go on." Dan nudged her arm. "Try it on."

"Will you be needing shoes, Fräulein? We need to know the correct length for the hem."

"No. I bought ballroom dancing shoes in New York, and fortunately they were packed in my big suitcase." She fished them out of her bag, then handed Dan the bag.

Hans and the seamstress unfastened the gown and lifted it carefully from the mannequin. "Now, if your handsome prince would care to have a seat, we can try this on for size."

"We?" Dan mouthed.

She winced. "Will you please just sit down and stay out of trouble for five minutes?"

****

It was considerably more than five minutes, and the seamstress scurried from the dressing room to a secluded part of the shop a few times, returning with several tiny garments she shielded from Dan's curious gaze. He smothered a laugh.

It's not like I haven't seen it all before. Or picked it up off the floor.

Finally, Lacey emerged from the fitting room,

holding the skirt carefully so she wouldn't trip.

"What do you think?" She stepped up on a little raised platform in the center of a semicircle of mirrors and turned so he could see the full effect.

The dark blue gown sparkled subtly under the bright lights. The color set off her fair skin and blue eyes perfectly. Her golden hair tumbled loose around her bare shoulders—a delightful blend of formal and footloose that was just so...*Lacey*.

"Dan?"

"I think...if I wasn't already head over heels in love with you, that dress just might do the trick."

Her cheeks flushed rosy and she glanced down, then up through her lashes. All of which had him wishing they were back at their hotel, sans audience.

Hans and the seamstress eyed the gown's fit and conferred in hushed tones. He nodded and shooed the seamstress toward the platform. She knelt and started pinning the hem.

"Fräulein, with this gown, I guarantee you'll have no shortage of partners at the ball."

Lacey met Dan's gaze with the tiniest hint of a smirk. "I only need one."

Chapter Twenty

Dan's arm protested sightly at being guided into a sleeve, but Lacey didn't need to know that. He kept his eyes shut as a comforting weight settled over his shoulders and the warm smell of new leather filled his nostrils. "Can I look yet?"

"Okay—go ahead." She stepped back, hands clasped under her chin, obviously unsure of his reception of her gift.

As if there could ever be any question.

Supple black leather, plenty of inside pockets—the monogrammed blue silk lining was a new twist, but it was remarkably similar to his dearly departed jacket. "I love it."

"Really?"

"Really."

"I tried to get it as close as possible—"

He stepped closer and wrapped his arms around her—twinges be damned. "I love it." He leaned down and brushed her lips softly with his own.

She relaxed in his arms. "Well, you really couldn't keep running around without a jacket at this time of year."

"Especially here. There're so many places where cars are prohibited. That was not a fun stroll yesterday."

"I'm sorry. I hoped it would be here—"

Her spine tensed beneath his fingers, and he ran his

hand up and down her back until she softened against him again.

"Stop it. You have exactly zero control over delivery services at Christmas."

"There's gloves in the pocket."

"So there are." He slipped them on—buttery soft and a perfect fit. "Whatever can I do to repay such magnanimity?"

She twined her arms around his neck, grinning impudently. "Oh, I'm sure we'll think of something. What else do you need to replace?"

"One of my shirts and my green wool sweater."

"So I suppose you'll be wanting the navy one back?"

He shook his head with a fond smile. "Eventually, yes—it's one of my favorites. But—and don't let this go to your head—you're right about the cardigan being easier to get on and off right now. So now that I'm properly outfitted, what's on the agenda for today?"

Lacey actually bounced a bit on her feet. "A tour of the Spanish Riding School."

"The city girl wants to see dancing horses?"

"They take you into the stable and everything."

Her eyes shone and she vibrated with excitement…and he couldn't resist teasing, just a little.

He wrinkled his nose. "You know stables smell, right?"

"I don't think this one does. From what I understand, it's like the royal palace of stables."

"And it's full of horses. No matter how pretty it is, a horse still—"

She made a pouty face and he leaned in and kissed her again, tasting a smudge of powdered sugar on the corner of her mouth. *I could do this all day. Do we really have to go out?*

"All right, all right—we'll go see where the pretty dancing horsies live."

"I knew you'd see it my way."

****

Lacey nudged him with her elbow. "If this is the ballroom for horses, what's the people one gonna be like?"

He snorted, taking in the crystal chandeliers and elaborate displays of holiday greenery decorating the balustrades. "Less sand, I hope."

She eyed him thoughtfully. "You act like you've never seen this before."

"In a way, I haven't. I'm seeing it all fresh through your eyes. I don't think I've ever just…let myself go and appreciated what's around me."

It was an odd sensation, paying attention to the facts and figures of a literal palace built for horses, not focusing on exits and security measures, although he noted a fire door, four cameras, and a uniformed security guard, all the same. He suspected that awareness would never truly desert him—it had kept him safe for far too long. And knowing he'd be returning to the hotel in the evening with Lacey, not venturing out in search of easy marks, was equal parts comforting and arousing.

She tugged gently on his good arm as they followed the guide through to the tack room and stables. "You okay? No headache?"

"I'm fine. You having fun?"

"I am. I—oh, wow."

Wow, indeed.

The white stallions were much larger up close, towering over Lacey. *I've never been so glad to see a fence between me and the valuables.* Was it possible for horses to look self-satisfied? These certainly did. Then again, if he'd been born and raised in an Alpine pasture, then transferred to luxurious quarters in an imperial palace, with the promise of a *very* happy retirement and a private harem to follow, he'd probably be pretty happy with his lot.

He glanced at Lacey, sparkling with excitement as she asked their guide a question.

Harems are overrated. I've got her.

****

A short walk found them back in the high-end shopping district. There were more cameras here, as well as officers patrolling the cobblestone streets. Some shops had private security—understandable, considering the array of haute couture boutiques, not to mention the fine jewelry establishments. Although the tiny petit point shop could probably give most of them a run for their money in terms of cash on hand.

Let it go. It's a beautiful day. Just enjoy it.

Unlike the malls at home, which would be a depressing mix of clearance signs, denuded displays, and decorations in the process of being torn down in favor of garish Valentine's Day crap, here, the opulent greenery and lights remained in place. People weren't making a mad scramble to return gifts either. It was refreshing.

Here, in the open plaza, Lacey walked on his injured side—not that he had any valuables within reach of a pickpocket.

"Nice police presence," she noted, scanning the area.

He offered a one-shouldered shrug. "There's a lot of money concentrated here."

"And a lot of tourists with big mouths and social media accounts."

He made a noncommittal noise, perusing the shop windows.

Menswear...good. And that shop looks perfect for—

A startled yelp dragged his attention back to Lacey.

"Oh my goodness, young man! You should be more aware of your surroundings." Her tone dripped saccharine, but there was a certain feral edge to her smile.

The punk whose foot she'd stomped on scowled and slunk off into the crowd.

Dan chuckled. " 'Young man?' He doesn't really look that much younger than you."

She glared after him. "Little shit. I am *done* with people trying to ruin my holiday. Now come on. We've got some shopping to do."

****

The dance class everyone said was so enjoyable? Not so much. Not when his arm felt like it was slowly being twisted out of the socket. Any hopes he'd had of hovering on the sidelines and maybe swaying a bit to the music were quickly disabused by the instructor. American slow dancing wouldn't cut it at one of these shindigs. At least they weren't trying any lifts or other foolishness. He'd never forgive himself if he dropped Lacey or hurt her through his clumsiness.

Dammit, I'm in good shape. It's just dancing.

His arm throbbed, and he winced. He couldn't help it. He hated not being at his best, and he hated the worry in Lacey's eyes, and he really hated the damn instructor and his cheerful voice.

Lacey tried to compensate, and one of the teaching

179

assistants quickly maneuvered her back into the correct position. She frowned at him, and he tried to release the tension from his shoulders.

"Babe? Do you need to rest?"

I need a handful of painkillers and the damn sling. How does my arm hurt worse now than it did the day I was shot?

"I'm fine."

"You're full of it."

He straightened his back and guided her through a turn, ignoring the burn in his muscles. "Think we're ready for one of those reality TV dancing shows?"

The instructor clapped his hands. "Now that you have the basic steps, we'll speed up the tempo to half-time."

He groaned.

****

Warm air enveloped them when they stepped into the blue-and-cream elegance of the hotel lobby. Lacey sniffed—the rich scents of coffee and chocolate were enticing, especially after their exertions in the dance studio.

"Come on—let's check out the café. I want one of those enormous slices of chocolate cake."

Dan chuckled as he guided her with a hand on her back. "Of course you do."

The desk clerk waved when she saw them. "Fräulein Devere, we have just sent a delivery to your suite."

"The airport found my bag?"

The clerk checked her computer. "No, I am afraid not. It was from a local couturier. It was delivered by hand, on a hanger, so we took the liberty of sending it straight up and placing it in the closet."

"Excellent. Thank you."

"And Herr Lewis, the valet returned your tuxedo as well."

He smiled at Lacey. "Looks like we're all set for the ball."

"Now can I *please* get that chocolate cake?"

Chapter Twenty-One

Dan lounged in the doorway, fastening his cuffs…or trying to. His fingers wouldn't cooperate with the studs.

"Here—let me do that." Lacey fastened the French cuffs for him, then did up his collar. "Want me to fix your tie?"

"Please."

She straightened the black silk-satin tie around his neck and knotted it, smoothing it with a proprietary hand.

So close in his personal space, he smelled the floral scent of her bubble bath and whatever product the hotel stylist had used on her hair. The blue gown hugged her figure perfectly, sparkling under the chandelier.

Breathtaking…as always.

Which made his next words more difficult to get out. "So, you may have noticed a lack of formal gifts on my part."

She pulled his vest from the hanger. "Dan, I thought we agreed we weren't going to be those people who make themselves crazy trying to manufacture the perfect holidays?"

"I know, but…I wanted this Christmas to be special."

She rolled her eyes. "Special is one way of putting it. But really…even with all the craziness…it's us, you know?" She stepped behind him and helped slide his arms into the vest, then darted around and buttoned it for him.

"It is, indeed. Still, I got this for you at the boutique. I thought it would go with your dress." He fished a tiny box from his pocket and passed it over.

The box contained a pair of delicate crystal teardrop earrings, midnight blue to match her gown. "They're perfect." She kissed his cheek. "Thank you."

He held the box while she slipped the earrings in. "What do you think?"

The stones glimmered with her movements, like the beading on her dress. "I think I may need a baseball bat to beat off all the guys who are gonna wanna cut in."

"Suppose I don't want to let anyone cut in?"

"Not sure how polite that is," he chuckled.

"Not sure how much I care." She smoothed her dress. "I've got something for you, too. It just—"

"Hasn't arrived yet?"

She flushed and toyed with the edge of his vest. "I had an idea, but I didn't know where to get it, then I was worried about delivery, and then—"

"Stuff happened."

She huffed out a mirthless little laugh. "And kept happening."

"You know, that sounds an awful lot like what I was going to say." He slid his good arm around her waist and skidded his fingertips over the tiny beads on her dress.

"Anyway, I just ordered it the other day when we were shopping. I hope it's delivered in time."

He stepped away from his comfy doorframe, tightening his grip on Lacey's waist. "Well, you know, in this part of the world, Christmas goes on until the sixth of January. Some places don't even give big gifts until then."

She set her hand on his shoulder and stepped back slightly, like they'd practiced in the dance class. "Yes, but we'll be leaving before then. And the way this trip has gone, I'd like to know it's safely in our possession."

"As long as it says Dolce Vita on the label, I'm pretty sure the company can forward it to us." He took another step, guiding her into a turn, albeit not as smoothly as he'd prefer.

She smiled at him. "Do you really want to trust our luck?"

"Our luck is pretty damn good, if you ask me." *Oh, this is gonna sound so sappy…what the hell…* "Of all the people in this world, we found each other. If that's not lucky, I don't know what is." He pulled her closer, and she supported his bad arm with her free hand.

"And all the crazy?"

"Doesn't matter."

"Some of it matters. Choosing to have a kid or jump in front of a bullet—those things matter."

"They do. And those are the things we'll work through—together. But stupid stuff—broken thermostats and lost bags and crazy sports fans—those don't matter. Those're just funny stories we'll tell someday."

She stretched up on her toes, angling for a kiss, then jumped as someone knocked loudly on the door of their suite.

"Deliveries for Fräulein Devere and Herr Lewis."

Lacey quirked an eyebrow. "Both of us?"

"Sounds like it." He headed for the door, fishing a couple of euros from his pocket for a tip, and returned a moment later with two small shopping bags emblazoned with the name of the same shop. "So this is what was happening when you 'needed to use the restroom' the

184

other day?" He passed her the one with her name on it.

She nodded, eyes sparkling as she pulled a small box from her bag and then extended it to him.

He bounced an identical box in his hand. "These boxes look suspiciously similar."

Lacey's cheeks flushed pink. "They do, don't they?"

"Am I about to be accused of 'going all caveman?'"

"Well, I don't really have a leg to stand on this time. Go on...open it." They traded boxes. Her blush deepened, and she caught her lower lip between her teeth.

He opened his, revealing a wide silver band engraved with numbers. "Coordinates?"

She nodded. "It's the GPS location of the hotel elevator in Madrid where I first met you. I knew I wanted to get to know you. I just never dreamed we'd end up here."

He tried the ring on a couple of fingers, finally working it over the knuckle and settling it on his right ring finger.

"I had to guess the size," Lacey confessed. "We can have it adjusted—"

He leaned in and stole the words from her lips with a kiss. "It's perfect." Another kiss. "Open yours."

Another wide silver band. Another set of coordinates. She looked up, tears shimmering in her eyes.

Dan took the ring and slid it onto the third finger of her right hand. "I didn't guess. I 'borrowed' the cocktail ring you wear when you get dressed up and had them match the size." He stroked his thumbs over her hand. His throat worked for a moment before he spoke. "These are the coordinates of a hotel room in London. A room where you saw me for who I really am...and you wouldn't let me walk away."

She tipped her head, studying him. "Are you proposing?"

"Are you?"

She chewed her lip. "I don't think so. I don't think we're there yet. This is a reminder of how we got here. Okay?"

He dislodged her lip with his thumb and pressed his lips to hers. "It's perfect. Neither of us is quite the same person who stepped into that elevator in Madrid."

"And neither of us would be who we are today without the other. Before I met you, I never dreamed I'd enjoy seeing an opera or spending a whole day in a museum. Thank you for..."

"Seeing more than everyone else did?"

She nodded.

"That's what you did for me. I have a job and a future—"

"And a penchant for jumping in front of guns."

"You're never gonna let me live that down, are you?"

"Nope." She looked at their intertwined hands. "For what it's worth, I'd love to have Dylan for a sister someday. If you're willing to share."

"I'd love to have a dad someday. If you're willing to share.

"I think that can be arranged."

"Are you absolutely sure we have to go out tonight?"

"After we went to so much trouble to get me a dress and learn the dance? I think we kinda have to." She smoothed his tie and straightened his vest. "It's another story to tell, right? How we danced the night away at a grand ball in a palace?"

"We could just invent something."

****

Lacey watched the activity through the windows of the motor coach. Crowds of happy people thronged the pavement. Impromptu dance parties surrounded stages scattered throughout the city. "There's a lot going on out there."

"That's the *Silvesterpfad*. It's sort of like a big block party. People follow the trail from stage to stage. There's different bands and I think even a waltz lesson at one stop."

"It looks like fun." The scene outside seemed much livelier than the aura of sedate formality inside the motor coach.

"I think we're a bit overdressed."

"Or underdressed, depending on your criteria. But maybe we could come back another year and do that?"

"We could."

"Will they play 'Auld Lang Syne' at midnight?"

"Traditionally, it's a quadrille."

"Which is?"

"Sort of a precursor of square dancing. Someone calls out the steps."

"In German? I don't think I could manage that."

"It gets a bit silly. It's not like the waltz that people expect you to perform perfectly. Or at least competently."

****

Lacey glanced over the balcony into the ballroom below. The murmur of hundreds of voices mingled with the discordant jangle of an orchestra warming up.

Enormous gilt-framed mirrors lined the walls, reflecting the glittering lights of crystal chandeliers. She squeezed Dan's arm. "I can't believe people actually lived here once."

"You finally get to attend a ball in the palace where Marie Antoinette was born and Mozart played for the Empress. Does it live up to your expectations?"

"It's amazing." They passed sumptuous flower arrangements set in alcoves on plinths as tall as she was. "I don't have to try to attract the eye of the handsome prince—I've already got mine." She twined her hands around his arm.

He smiled and rolled his shoulder unobtrusively. "You know, if I can't keep up, you should go ahead and dance with anyone who asks. I want you to enjoy yourself."

She shot him a look. "I want to spend the evening with you."

The luxurious scarlet carpet runner muffled their steps as they descended the grand staircase to the gleaming parquet dance floor. An usher bowed and escorted their group to the Dolce Vita tables.

"How does this work, exactly?" she wondered, slipping into her seat.

Fluffy Pink Bathrobe Lady from Amsterdam leaned across the table, dressed in an equally pink ballgown. Her silver hair was elegantly coiffed, and she exuded a choking smog of French perfume. "The master of ceremonies will present this evening's group of debutantes. They'll perform a specially choreographed dance with their escorts. The phrase you listen for is 'Alles Walzer!' That means we can all dance." She eyed Dan and Lacey speculatively, lingering on their obviously-not-wedding rings. "Is this your first Viennese ball, dear?"

Lacey nodded.

"I thought as much. I noticed your young man struggling a bit in the class. If he needs to take a break, there are always highly skilled gentlemen available to make sure no young lady is disappointed."

Does she even know what that sounds like? Under the cover of the table, Dan squeezed her hand. *Okay...he heard that the same way I did.*

"Well, I want to spend the evening with my friend, but, um...thanks."

"Of course, dear." She turned and spoke quietly to her husband, a portly gentleman with thick glasses and a comb-over. Then she whispered to the matron on her other side, who glanced at them, then turned to her own husband.

Dan draped his good arm over the back of Lacey's chair and leaned in with a seductive smile. His warm breath tickled her ear. "I don't think I like the look of that."

She glanced down through her lashes, lips curved as if he'd murmured sweet nothings. "Not sure I do, either."

Mrs. Pink sighed nostalgically. "I wish I could have made my debut at a ball like this. Of course, the Cotillion in New York City was lovely, but just think of making your debut at an imperial palace! Mother and I flew to Paris on the Concorde to order my gown."

Her neighbor spoke with a wistful Southern accent. "Mine was in Washington, DC. Papa was stationed at the Pentagon, and he wore his evening dress uniform when he presented me. There's nothing quite like a Marine officer with white gloves and his chest full of medals."

Her husband, who frankly didn't look like he'd ever worn a uniform in his life, never looked up from his phone.

Me in a poufy white dress? Dad in his NYPD dress blues? Not in this universe.

She tried adding a veil to the mental image.

Nope. Still not happening.

The former Southern belle smiled graciously at Lacey. "What about you, dear? Which ball did you attend?"

Crap. Crappity crap crap. She does not wanna hear about the junior prom at a high school in the Bronx.

Fortunately, an earsplitting trumpet fanfare heralded the opening of the festivities. A double line of impossibly young white-gowned debs escorted by equally young gentlemen in white tie and tails processed down the steps. A few speakers made remarks, and then the conductor raised his baton.

The dancers bowed and curtsied to one another, then launched into a carefully rehearsed dance that seemed a hybrid of ballet and the formal waltz they'd practiced at the dance school. Red ribbon streamers flowing from the nosegay each girl held punctuated the sea of swirling white gowns. The music built to a crescendo, and the young men lifted their partners in a series of increasingly daring aerials.

It was lovely to watch, but the idea of Dan, with a bum arm, or any of the older gentlemen seated at their table attempting to lift anyone was just—no. *So much no.* She reached for her champagne glass to stifle the snickers threatening to erupt.

She glanced sidewise at Dan, and yup—his lips were pressed together, and his expression was more or less impassive, but she could see a muscle jumping in his cheek. Still, it was a beautiful display, straight out of a fairy tale.

The dancers concluded their routine and curtsied and bowed to thunderous applause. Someone was speaking, but the words were lost in a sea of scuffling as gentlemen got to their feet and held their partner's chairs.

Dan slid his arm out of the sling and flexed it a couple of times, wincing.

"Are you okay?"

"I'll be fine. We're at a ball, right? Gotta dance the first waltz with my best girl." He winked and extended his arm.

She slid her arm through his, and they strolled to the dance floor, which rapidly filled to capacity.

"Why don't we stay on the edge, in case we need to sit down?" she suggested.

"The outside of the floor is the fast lane. We might be better off—"

The master of ceremonies announced, "*Alles Walzer!*" and the orchestra struck up a lively waltz. Couples whirled into the dance, sucking them into the maelstrom.

Dan kept his arms raised to the correct height and guided her through the steps with almost his usual level of grace and expertise.

Almost.

Fine lines appeared on his forehead and the corner of his mouth puckered. A tremor ran through his bad arm. The second time another couple jostled them, Lacey took matters into her own hands. She squeezed his hand and steered them off the dance floor.

"Come on…let's sit down."

She led him back to their table and helped him guide his arm into the sling. He slumped into his chair and the tense lines smoothed out of his face.

"I'm sorry."

"I'm not. You got hurt saving a man's life—saving a family—for Christmas. That's so much more important than a stupid dance."

"I know, but it's our first Christmas together and I just wanted one thing to go right."

"Hey—we're at a ball at an imperial palace. That's pretty cool if you ask me."

"Yeah, but we're sitting on the sidelines."

She shrugged. "Now, we've got a couple of choices. We can dance with you hurting—but I'm not okay with that. We can sit here and drink champagne and comment on everyone's dancing skills. Or lack thereof."

"You'll have to dodge a lot of invitations if we do that. Any other options?"

"Or we can go outside and join in the sil—silver—the street party."

Dan chuckled. "The *Silvesterpfad*."

"That."

"If we do, we should stop at the hotel and change first. People go out for street food after balls all the time, but I think we'll get cold pretty fast dressed like this."

"Fine. Let's go." She glanced back at the dance floor and saw the pink lady towing her husband in their direction. "Come on, before I get stuck with an old guy stomping all over my toes."

"Are you sure you want to leave after just half a dance? It's your first ball, and we had all the adventure of finding you a new dress. Which is beyond stunning, by the way."

"You should know. You picked it." She grinned and gave him a saucy wink. "We came, we saw, we danced—on our own terms. I'm good." She held out a hand and pulled him to his feet.

He leaned down and kissed her lightly on the lips. "As my lady wishes."

****

It took time to skirt the dance floor and work their way to the coat room. Although the bulk of the crowd pranced through a polka, there were still plenty of couples taking breaks and waiters circulating with round silver trays of champagne flutes. Dan spoke to the Dolce Vita rep about a car while Lacey collected her wrap.

The doorman bowed from the neck as he held the door for them. Outside, Lacey closed her eyes and drew in a refreshing breath of cool, crisp, almost-midnight air. Cars whooshed by on the street and echoes of music from the stages drifted on the breeze.

Dan slid his good arm around her waist. "Okay, babe?"

She wrinkled her nose. "There were just too many flowers and perfumes going on in there."

They strolled to the valet stand. The valet captain, bundled up in an old-fashioned caped greatcoat, bowed and tipped his top hat to them.

"The car should be here in a few minutes. Are you warm enough?"

She slid her arms around him. "You can keep me warm while we wait."

"What will you tell Mrs. Wilson when she asks about the ball?"

"The truth. We went, it was very lovely, and maybe we'll try it again sometime."

He pulled her a bit closer, and they swayed to the faint strains of music. "So, is this gonna be our thing?"

"What's that?"

"Escaping when things get too formal."

"We've done lots of formal things—the opera, the ballet."

"And we've run out on a few."

"Like what?"

"Like that dinner in Italy."

"They put a plate of octopus in front of me!" She shuddered. "A whole octopus! It had tentacles and suckers and…stuff. I think it was looking at me."

"The fashion museum gala?"

"That guy was talking about how people in the Middle Ages collected pee to get ammonia to process wool. You're lucky I didn't toss all your sweaters in the charity bin. Anyway, those weren't so much a question of formality as just plain not fun. And if this crazy mess of a trip has taught me anything, it's that life is too short to sit through meals you don't like or experiences that just don't hold any meaning for you when there's so much to see. Tonight didn't work out, for a lot of reasons. I'm willing to try again. How about you?"

"Not all balls are so formal, you know. There are costume balls and ones where people wear traditional Alpine clothing."

She allowed her gaze to track him from head to toe. "You, in those short leather pants? I could go for that."

He returned the perusal—with interest. "Well, you know what sort of dress you'd be wearing, right? Fluffy skirts and a lace-up bodice? I could go for that."

She leaned against his shoulder, her face scrunched with laughter…and then she jumped at a sound like artillery fire.

Fireworks blossomed into a riot of glittering colors over the palace and people cheered. Every church bell in the city tolled in the New Year.

Dan chuckled. "Guess I lost track of time."

"You?"

"I've told you before—you're distracting." He leaned down, intent clear in his blue eyes. "Happy New Year, Lacey."

"Happy New Year, Dan." She shifted up on the balls of her feet and met him halfway. His lips were warm and soft against hers. His arm around her made her feel safe and cherished.

Fireworks continued to burst overhead, filling the sky with color and the air with the stench of cordite.

The kiss continued a bit beyond the bounds of propriety. It might have continued longer, but Dan's inside jacket pocket started vibrating. As did Lacey's wristlet. They broke apart, slightly breathless.

He liberated his phone first. "It's the hotel."

He accepted the call while Lacey fumbled hers out.

"Herr Lewis, we are delighted to inform you Fräulein Devere's bag has just been delivered."

She thumped her head against his shoulder. "Perfect timing."

A word about the author...

I am an author with a penchant for writing about strong, sassy ladies and the men they love (and cats!). I have a background in historic and theatrical costuming. I live in New York with my cat, Miss Toby Toebeanz, and lots and lots of books and Legos. My debut novel, Picture Imperfect, was released in March 2023. https://www.pinterest.com/kateberberichauthor/

Thank you for purchasing
this publication of The Wild Rose Press, Inc.

For questions or more information
contact us at
info@thewildrosepress.com.

The Wild Rose Press, Inc.
www.thewildrosepress.com